The Root

of all

Trouble

Heather Webber

Other books by Heather:

As Heather Webber

The Nina Quinn Mystery Series
A Hoe Lot of Trouble
Trouble in Spades
Digging up Trouble
Trouble in Bloom
Weeding out Trouble
Trouble Under the Tree
The Root of all Trouble

The Lucy Valentine Novels
Truly, Madly
Deeply, Desperately
Absolutely, Positively
Perfectly Matched

The River of Dreams Historical Romances
Surrender, My Love
Secrets of the Heart
Hearts are Wild

As Heather Blake

The Wishcraft Mysteries
It Takes a Witch
A Witch Before Dying
The Good, the Bad, and the Witchy

The Magic Potion Mysteries
A Potion to Die For

The Root of All Trouble
Copyright © 2013 Heather Webber
www.heatherwebber.com

ISBN-13: 978-1484816783

ISBN-10: 1484816781

Chapter One

Thou, Nina Colette Ceceri Quinn, from now on will heed severe weather warnings despite the complete unreliability of local meteorologists.

Black clouds loomed overhead and hail pounded my truck as I took a left out of my office's parking lot. The self-important weatherman on Channel 13 had been gleeful this morning as he warned about possible thunderstorms, straight-line winds, and tornadoes.

I hadn't believed him. Mostly because he'd been warning of the same thing for the past two weeks and nothing had come from it except for a few sprinkles.

Late springtime in this area was, as a rule, unpredictable.

I'd lived in Freedom, Ohio, a growing suburb just north of Cincinnati, nearly my whole life and had been affected by truly severe weather only a couple of times.

But after seeing those telltale clouds, I vowed to never take the forecast of impending doom lightly again. Once a commandment, always a commandment.

"Pouting doesn't become you," I said to my employee Jean-Claude Reaux.

His car was in the shop, and he was hitching a ride with me to meet up with his cousins—whose construction company happened to be working across the street from my house.

I regretted making the offer of riding with me.

Sitting in the passenger seat with his arms crossed over his chest, he flexed his muscles in an attempt to cheer himself up. "Don't talk crazy, Nina. Everything becomes me."

"Silly me," I teased at his serious tone.

This storm was shaping up to be one of the worst I'd seen. I sent all my employees at Taken by Surprise, Garden Designs home when the hail started. Even though we weren't working an outdoor jobsite today, I didn't want to take chances with the weather and their safety.

Plus, it was Friday, and we'd all been more than ready to go home. We'd been in planning meetings all day for our upcoming makeover of my new neighbors' back yard, which was to take place this weekend. All-day meetings felt like a special form of torture, especially with my colorful crew. Don't get me wrong. I loved my formerly felonious employees, but there was only so much a girl could take before I felt the need to escape. Far, far away.

The early dismissal had come at the perfect time. Tension had been rising inside the office thanks to some good-natured ribbing gone wrong, and it was good to send everyone home before a fight broke out.

I didn't do well with bloodshed.

I'd seen a lot of it, too, over the past year, with all those homicide cases I'd been caught up in. I'd become a bit of a dead-body magnet. It wasn't a label I was proud of.

At the heart of the office tension was Jean-Claude and Kit Pipe, another long-time employee. Jean-Claude didn't like people teasing him—especially where his family was concerned, and Kit just couldn't help himself from poking fun—especially when there was such an easy target.

All it had taken was one crack from Kit and the rest of my employees had joined in, perfectly demonstrating a pack mentality. Jean-Claude should have known better than to take the joking personally, but he'd been on edge lately, and I hoped that didn't mean he was harboring a guilty conscience about some sneaky scheme or another. He was forever cooking up new schemes.

Shooting me a dirty look, Jean-Claude went back to flexing. He'd worked for me for years now, having come to my company the way most of my employees did: through my cousin, Analise Bertoli, whose job title had just changed. She used to be a county probation officer, but now she was a "correctional treatment specialist," a designation she had embraced so whole-heartedly that she promptly ordered new business cards.

Speaking of Ana...I peeked in the rearview mirror, and saw Kit, my second-in-command, driving behind me in his big bad Hummer. He and Ana had been dating for a while now and were quite serious. He'd been pressuring her to move in with him, but she was holding out for an engagement ring before that kind of commitment. I wished he'd hurry up and ask. I liked the two of them together. A lot. It made perfect sense that Kit was following me so closely—he lived directly across the street from my small bungalow and was on his way home as well.

Thunder cracked overhead, and as much as I wanted to press the gas pedal to the floorboard, I forced myself to creep down the road. Water covered the asphalt, obscuring any dividing line, and visibility was only a few feet in front of the truck. What seemed like every piece of litter in the county flew by the windshield, *Wizard of Oz* style. I wouldn't have been the least bit surprised to see Miss Gulch on her bike whizz past. It was that kind of storm.

Glancing in the mirror, I noticed the dark circles under my muddy green eyes, and if those weren't bad enough, the rain had wreaked havoc with my hair. Strands of light brown stuck out every which way.

At nearly two in the afternoon the sky was as dark as night. Fast-moving clouds hugged the ground, murky fingers dipping low, swirling into funnel shapes. All it would take was one to touch the ground, and a tornado would be born.

Chewing the inside of my cheek, I worried about my sixteen-year-old stepson Riley, who was still in school this time of day—it was the last week of classes before summer break. The school wouldn't release the kids into this mess, so that was reassuring, but I would have felt better if he was home.

Though, really, the location of his "home" was as murky as

the swirling clouds. Technically, he lived with my ex-husband Kevin, but he spent a lot of time at my house in the Mill, an older, settled neighborhood of Freedom also known as the Gossip Mill.

I'd also been seeing a lot of Kevin—mostly because he went out of his way to see me. He wasn't quite wooing me, trying to win me back, but he was walking that line, testing those waters.

I didn't know what to think about that, so I tried not to. Most of the time. Hardly ever, really.

Okay, I'd been obsessing.

Sue me.

I pushed the gas pedal down a little more and tried to keep my mind occupied with something else, anything else, other than this storm. "You shouldn't be so sensitive," I said. "You know how they are."

"They" being my other employees. They were a crazy lot, but I loved them all like family.

Jean-Claude's wavy hair was pulled back into a ponytail at the nape of his neck. "I take talk of my family seriously. We have a reputation to uphold."

I gripped the steering wheel and concentrated on the road so I wouldn't laugh. Jean-Claude's family was one step removed from the Sopranos.

All right, they weren't that bad. Most of them, like Jean-Claude, were reformed. But the criminal tendencies were still there, underneath the pretty surfaces.

"This is all your fault," he said to me.

"How so?" I asked, lifting my foot off the gas as the truck started to hydroplane. *Almost home, almost home.* I let out a breath of relief as I felt the tires grip the road.

"They're your friends. You got me into this."

He wasn't referring to the other employees, though I did consider most of them friends. He meant Perry Owens and Mario Gibbens. I'd met the couple last year on the set of a reality TV show (long story), and Perry and I hit it off right away. Mario was still warming up to me—mostly because he considered me a bad influence on his partner.

Sheesh. Funny how a few murder cases could affect a reputation.

They'd recently moved out of the city and into my neighborhood. The Mill, once a geriatric demographic, was slowly turning more urban as younger people moved in and, well, the older people...died.

Some not from natural causes (also a long story—or stories, I should say).

Right around Christmastime, there had been a murder in the neighborhood. The house where it occurred had sat empty for months. The bank foreclosed, and Perry and Mario decided it was the perfect chance to put down roots in an up-and-coming neighborhood.

It helped that they bought the place for a fraction of its worth, because the murder had scared away all the other (sane) buyers. Perry and Mario had moved in a month ago and had

6

immediately started demolition. When they found themselves over their heads with the construction, they decided to hire help who promised up and down that the job would be done in two weeks.

"Whoa now," I said. "I believe you were the one who recommended your cousin's company as a contractor. I recall I tried to talk you out of it."

I'd tried to talk Perry and Mario out of it, too. But in this economy, they couldn't turn down Reaux Construction's bargain basement bid on the job. Work had started two weeks ago, and was supposed to be completed at the end of this week.

They were nowhere near done.

None of them could say I didn't warn them that hiring the company was a bad idea. A very, very bad idea. They were Reauxs, after all.

I hadn't been the least bit surprised by the delays or when, just two days ago, the company's lothario foreman, Joey Miller, went out for "lunch" and never came back. I thought the company, owned by Jean-Claude's cousins Delphine and Plum, was better off without the guy. He'd given me the heebies.

The cousins were why Jean-Claude was in his current snit.

There hadn't been a day since that Jean-Claude wasn't teased by his coworkers about his colorful kin. Delphine and Plum were...interesting. Everyone in my office had gotten to know them well because Perry and Mario's yard was the one we were making over this weekend. Our paths crossed a lot as my crew took measurements and worked up a design plan for the yard.

Ordinarily, Taken by Surprise specialized in *surprise* garden makeovers, but I could never turn down a friend in need of a backyard makeover—and Perry and Mario were in desperate need. Winter—not to mention the bank's neglect—hadn't been kind to their yard, not that it had ever been well-maintained.

I slowed to a stop at a red light and watched the traffic signal bounce in the wind. Rain slashed the windows, hail pounded, and I spotted trees uprooted all along the street. My pulse pounded in my ears and my palms began to sweat.

Jean-Claude gave up on flexing. "Just because my cousins look the way they do, dress the way they do, and talk the way they do doesn't mean that they can't get the job done. They and the rest of the crew will be done in no time."

Riiiiight. "Name one thing that's been completed there this week."

Wind buffeted the truck as I turned left, into the Mill. Trees were down in here, too, along with power lines. I steered the truck around broken branches.

His lips puckered. "Delphine and Plum are getting the lay of the land, a feel for the job, the energy of the house. Plus," he said, "Delphine can't find her favorite hammer and she's paralyzed without it."

"That's a bit dramatic. A hammer is a hammer."

He scoffed. "Said like a layman."

My calluses begged to differ, but I didn't want to argue.

"And their crew?" The ragtag group had been on the job since the beginning.

"They're just following orders." He shrugged.

I waited for him to realize this "method" wasn't normal, but he said nothing. Instead, he stared sullenly out the window. His mood was starting to get to me.

Fortunately, I had to tolerate only a few minutes more of Jean-Claude's poutiness before I could be rid of him, leaving him in the care of his *capable* cousins. I had big plans for the next hour or so that involved a flashlight, a roll of cookie dough, a storm radio, and an interior closet.

Cars and construction trucks lined the road as I neared Mario and Perry's house to drop off Jean-Claude. I pulled into the driveway and parked behind a big Dumpster. A bolt of lightning flashed and thunder quickly followed.

"What's going on there?" Jean-Claude asked.

A crowd had gathered in the back yard, getting soaked to the bone. "Looks like that ash tree finally came down." I'd been worried about that tree and warned Perry that it should be cut down before it fell down and possibly hurt someone or something, but he liked its height and the shade offered from its uppermost canopy.

No one listened to me anymore.

Luckily, the tree hadn't fallen on the house. It looked to have hit the ground and split in half, revealing its rotten innards. There was quite the gathering around its base.

Delphine, Plum and their crew were there, along with Perry, my neighbor Mr. Cabrera, and several other neighbors as well.

All but Delphine were getting soaked (she had an umbrella), and didn't seem to have a care in the world about the weather.

Perry glanced over his shoulder, saw my truck idling, and waved for me to come over.

He was a hairdresser by trade, and I had to wonder if he'd sniffed too many chemicals. He'd clearly lost his mind if he thought I was going out there with all that lightning.

I shook my head.

He waved again, more insistently. Mr. Cabrera joined in.

"You better go," Jean-Claude urged.

He was a fine one to volunteer me. "How about you go?"

"No way. Do you know what that rain will do to my hair?"

I gritted my teeth and threw the truck into park. Wishing I had a sweatshirt, I gave an oblivious Jean-Claude the Ceceri Evil Eye and hopped out into the rain.

Water dripped down my face as I sprinted toward Perry.

Above the wailing wind, I picked up another sound. At first I thought it was the tornado siren, but no...it was a regular siren and growing closer.

I glanced over my shoulder as a police car pulled up to the curb. Jean-Claude slunk in his seat, and I had to wonder if it was just a natural instinct on his part or if he'd gotten himself into trouble lately.

Perry reached out and grabbed my arm. "What kind of

neighborhood is this?"

Now he was asking that question? The murders here hadn't tipped him off earlier?

"What's going on?" I asked, fearing the tree had fallen on someone.

"Take a look, Miz Quinn." Mr. Cabrera's eyes were alight with excitement. There was nothing he liked more than a little hubbub in the neighborhood.

Leaning around him, I blinked at the sight before me—the sight that had captured everyone's attention. The broken tree had revealed something else besides its rotten core.

I moved in for a closer look at the upper half of a body that had partially fallen out of the broken trunk. I swallowed hard as I recognized the man.

Joey Miller had been found.

Chapter Two

"This is all your fault, Miz Quinn," Mr. Cabrera said, trying his best to give me his own form of an evil eye.

With his bushy white eyebrows snapped downward in a furry v-shape, he couldn't quite pull off the look. In fact, he looked so much like a Muppet that it was hard to take him seriously. He'd put on weight over the last few months, thanks to his girlfriend Ursula "Brickhouse" Krauss practically living with him and cooking his meals, and his cheeks had rounded out along with his belly. Both were jiggling, and the tummy wiggle made the pink flamingoes on his lime-green button-down appear to be doing the mamba. A pair of sensible khaki Bermuda shorts and leather sandals completed his outfit.

We stood in Perry and Mario's kitchen, staring out the sliding patio doors watching the goings-on of the police as they searched the yard. Rain continued to pour down. "How is this my fault?"

He threw a glance at Perry, who was rummaging through moving boxes searching for the hard liquor. I wasn't surprised that it hadn't been unpacked yet. Even though Mario and he liked the hooch more than anyone I knew (besides my mother and me), they didn't drink when they were counting calories. Now that it was bathing suit season they were constantly counting. I didn't know for sure, but I suspected Mario owned a Speedo or two.

Mr. Cabrera jabbed a finger in my direction. "This neighborhood has gone to seed since you moved in. Then your friends moved in. And now your friends are continuing *your* homicidal traditions. Next thing I know one of your family members will move into the house for sale next door to you and find a body in the basement."

"Homicidal traditions? I didn't commit any homicides...yet," I said, eyeing his chest like it had a big target on it. "And no one I know wants to move into that house. It's haunted."

The home, once owned by a granny panty thief, had been unable to hold a tenant for longer than a few weeks at a time. This was the fifth time it was for sale in a year.

"Everyone knows you're cursed," Mr. Cabrera pointed out, ignoring my jibe. "Apparently your friends are as well."

"Hey now," Perry said, pulling a pout.

He'd recently had some lip injections, so his pout was quite something.

"I'm hurt. Cut to the soul," Perry said dramatically. "I might die right here on the spot. Oh, wait. Is this spot already taken? Is this where Mr. Cabrera's *girlfriend* bit the dust last Christmas?" He blinked innocently, his gray-green eyes sparkling. "It seems to me I heard that Nina wasn't the only one around here who is cursed."

Folding his arms across his chest, Mr. Cabrera *harrumphed.*

"Perry has a good point," I said, finger-combing my wet hair. "Most of the deaths in this neighborhood have belonged to *your* lady friends."

Mr. Cabrera's curse involved his lady loves who tended to, ah, *expire* while dating him. Some by natural causes and some...not. This curse was why Brickhouse Krauss kept breaking up with him every few months—she was staying one step ahead of the Grim Reaper.

Technically, the woman who died in this house wasn't Mr. Cabrera's girlfriend at the time, but he'd been wooing her in hopes of making Brickhouse jealous, therefore the death was attributed to his curse.

"You weren't dating Joey Miller, were you, Mr. Cabrera?" Perry asked, wiggling his dirty blond, perfectly-shaped eyebrows. He took his manscaping seriously. "That might explain some things. Like your taste in shirts."

Perry, who was openly gay and had been since middle school, loved to tease Mr. Cabrera about his sexuality. At first, my grumpy meddling neighbor took it personally and went on the defensive. Now, however, he tended to tease right back.

His unruly eyebrows rose. "I may have passed along a compliment to him a time or two. He had a fine way with a circular saw. A true talent."

"Aha!" I accused playfully.

"Now, now, Miz Quinn," Mr. Cabrera said calmly. "As you well know, Ursula and I are doing just fine right now. This death," he waved toward the back yard, "is all on you and *your* curse."

It was true I had a bit of a reputation. I had an uncanny knack for finding dead bodies—people who'd been murdered—and for helping to solve their cases. At this point the police should just put me on the payroll.

Six months had passed since I'd seen any kind of dead body, and until today I had started to think my own curse was finally broken...

My curse, apparently, had been taking an extended vacation.

"That," I waved outside, "isn't my fault. I barely even knew him."

"Perry and Mario knew him," Mr. Cabrera said. "They're your friends, therefore you're guilty."

"And you've finally lost your mind," I said.

"Aha!" Perry pulled a bottle of gin from the box. He kissed the label before practically skipping toward the kitchen. "Who wants a G and T?"

"I do," Mr. Cabrera and I said at the same time.

It had been one of those days.

Dark clouds skimmed treetops as they sped eastward. It looked like the worst of the weather had passed. The Reaux Construction crew were still out in the elements, huddled together just beyond the deck, corralled by a police officer trying to keep them away from the crime scene. Delphine was the only one who had an umbrella and she wasn't sharing—the rest of them looked water-logged. A Freedom PD homicide detective would be here soon to talk to them.

I had a feeling I knew which one, too. Detective Kevin Quinn.

My ex-husband.

I couldn't escape the man.

And couldn't decide if I wanted to.

Lime slices balanced on tall glasses as Perry set the drinks on a fancy tray and carried them over to Mr. Cabrera and me. The tray was a nice touch of normal in the midst of all the dust and chaos. The walls had been torn down to the studs, the bricks from the fireplace lay in piles on the warped wooden floors, and the only furniture in the open living and dining room was a beat-up table with four mismatched chairs.

"Nice watch," I said, taking hold of his wrist. The vintage watch had a decorative golden crackled dial and a dark brown leather band.

"This is the one I told you about."

Perry had begun receiving anonymous gifts right after he moved in, and the watch was the latest to arrive. He'd yet to uncover the identity of his admirer. "It's a beauty."

Abandoning his drink for a moment, Perry stopped and admired the timepiece, holding his arm out to let the light glint off the crystal lens. "It's a shame I can only wear it when Mario is at work."

Mario was a court stenographer downtown, and I wondered if Mario was on his way home or if he was in a hearing and hadn't yet heard the news about Joey Miller.

"Why?" Mr. Cabrera took his drink off the tray.

"Because Mario thinks it's from an old boyfriend who's trying to get me back. He's the jealous type."

Mario, a dark-haired, dark-eyed Latino was definitely the jealous type.

"Could it be from an ex?" I asked.

"I don't think so. If any of my exes had this good of taste I'd probably still be with him."

Mr. Cabrera grunted. "A watch is a watch."

"Said the man with the flamingoes on his shirt," I said.

He raised his glass to me. "Said the woman with the *There's Something About Mary* hairdo."

My hands went to my hair and Perry knocked them away. "Let me." He twisted and tucked and next thing I knew, my hair was pulled up in some sort of chic knot.

Perry was a magician, I was convinced, his hair brush his magic wand.

As my stylist, he knew my hair better than anyone else. Maybe even better than I knew it myself. Until I met him I hadn't cared much about my hairstyle. Now I was in his chair getting highlights every eight weeks—my one vanity.

Mr. Cabrera frowned. "You don't have any idea who's sending the gifts?"

"None. I also got a silk pocket square and some expensive cologne. Mario doesn't know about those, so if we can keep them between us, I'd appreciate it."

"I can be persuaded," Mr. Cabrera said.

Perry sighed. "Which one do you want?"

"The cologne. The ladies love a great smelling man."

"You're making me queasy," I said. "Besides, why do you need to impress 'the ladies' when you have Mrs. Krauss?"

"I have a right to smell good, Miz Quinn," he snapped.

I rolled my eyes and grabbed my drink. I had a feeling I'd need a refill soon.

Perry motioned toward the back yard. "I hate to think about how long he's been out there." He cocked a hip, swirled his ice, and said, "I started smelling something bad back there yesterday but couldn't figure out what it was. I thought it was a neighbor's trash. Mario joked that we'd moved into a trashy neighborhood."

"That's not funny," Mr. Cabrera said. "This neighborhood was just fine until—"

"Yeah, yeah," I said. "We don't need to go through all that again." I leaned on the edge of the table, and was glad that Mario wasn't home, or he would have chastised me to use a chair. He was a stickler like that.

Mr. Cabrera squeezed his lime. His dark eyes were as big as moonpies when he asked, "Did you see how his head was dented in like Mario's car that one time you crashed it?"

Despite his commentary about the state of the Mill, there was nothing Mr. Cabrera liked better than a little commotion in the neighborhood. He was the gossip king, and all this hubbub would be great fodder at his weekly to-do, which once included a cribbage match or a poker game. On tap this week was a Scrabble tournament.

"Makes sense," Perry said, "considering, and thanks for bringing up the car, Mr. C. Mario still gets peeved about that. See if I share that cologne with you after all."

"Considering what?" I asked, my nosiness at an all-time high.

"The bloody rhinestone hammer that fell out of the tree with the body. I'm guessing it was what did that to his skull." Perry *tsk*ed and said mournfully, "It's a shame, really. He had such a nice head of hair. Not many men can wear a shag cut and pull it off. That's about the only nice thing I can say about him."

Mr. Cabrera nodded in agreement. "The shag is a toughie. I tried it once in the seventies."

Perry gasped. "With your bone structure?"

"It was a mistake I've never repeated."

"Your Clark Cable slick suits you. Don't fix what ain't broke."

Mr. Cabrera patted his hair with a smug smile. I didn't think his 'do was in danger of change since he had a cabinet full of pomade at home that he wouldn't want to go to waste.

Sadly, I couldn't argue with Perry's assessment of Joey. The man was a bit of a...cretin. He'd pinched my ass more than a few times, and he leered at every woman he ever met. There was an air of slimeball about him that made me squirm. He was the type to steal a granny's retirement fund and milk from a baby.

It hadn't surprised me at all that he was dead.

What did surprise me was where he was found.

I stood up and peered out the slider. I hadn't seen the hammer when I arrived. "Wait a second. That hammer... Wasn't that Delphine's?"

"Have you ever seen anything more ridiculous?" Mr. Cabrera shook his head. "A rhinestone encrusted hammer?"

I was about to mention his shirt again, but decided against it and took another sip of my drink.

Jean-Claude mentioned the hammer had gone missing, but he neglected to mention it had gone missing at the same time as Joey.

"Do you think she's the one that bashed in his head?" Perry asked, his eyes aglow.

He was going to fit into this neighborhood just fine.

"I can't see it," Mr. Cabrera said. "She has the fight in her all right, but she's too tiny to get him into the tree."

"*On her own,*" Perry said ominously.

Mr. Cabrera nodded. "True, true."

"I wouldn't rule her out. The opening of that hollow was only three feet off the ground, and she's stronger than she looks."

Through the glass, I studied Delphine as she hunkered beneath a plain black umbrella. She was small, maybe five foot one or two, but she was as curvy as any 1940's pinup girl. She had long dark hair and smoky black eyes. A skintight black leather micro-mini skirt clung to her wide hips and nipped in at her narrow waist, and a tight t-shirt barely contained her double Ds. One of her crew members, Bear Broward, held the umbrella over her head, and she kept dabbing at her heavily-lined eyes with a tissue.

There was a don't-mess-with-me look about her that made me believe she wouldn't think twice about using that hammer on someone. But why? "Okay, conspiracy theorists, why would Delphine kill Joey? What's her motive? And wouldn't she have been stupid to leave the hammer behind?" She struck me as a lot of things but stupid wasn't one of them.

Perry finished off his drink and wiggled his eyebrows. "They were a couple."

"A couple of what?" Mr. Cabrera asked.

Perry shot him a look.

I said, "He can't handle his alcohol. It makes him loopy."

"A couple." Perry made kissing noises. "I saw them making out in the front seat of her truck once. Could be this head bashing is the result of a lover's quarrel."

"I like it," Mr. Cabrera slurred, making kissing sounds.

Perry pried the glass from his hand and said, "Ooh, here comes someone who can probably sort it all out. Man, does he get more gorgeous every day?"

Yes. Yes, he did. Not that I noticed or anything.

Kevin had arrived, and he didn't look too happy about the scene before him. A scowl tugged at his lips as rain spilled down his face.

"Don't let Mario hear you talking like that," I said, hating the pangs I felt in my stomach.

Perry made the sign of the cross.

Kevin looked around, then swiped a hand through his wet hair, slicking it back. He turned his face up toward the sky and Perry and I both sighed a little.

Mr. Cabrera knocked on the slider and waved like a madman, alerting Kevin to our presence inside the house. The dry house.

I said, "No more gin for him. Ever."

"You should have warned me before."

"I was a little distracted with the dead guy and all."

"They're coming up here," Mr. Cabrera said.

"I need a refill," Perry mumbled.

"Me, too. In a to-go cup." I needed to get out of here ASAP.

Perry grabbed my arm. "Oh no. You're the one who talked me into moving to this neighborhood in the first place. You're staying."

"If I'm staying," Mr. Cabrera said, "I'm going to need a refill, too."

"No," I said.

"You're not the boss of me, Miz Quinn." Mr. Cabrera set his hands on his hips and tipped his head, challenging me.

"Do I need to go and get Ursula?"

He paused for a second before grumbling, "She's not the boss of me, either."

"She's not?" This was news to me.

"She thinks she is, but she's not."

Perry said, "When are you going to pop the big question to Ursula anyhow? I thought you've been looking at engagement rings."

Mr. Cabrera sniffed. "I don't know if I am."

"What's that mean?" It had been decided that the key to them staying together permanently was to get married. His curse only affected women he *dated*.

"If you must know, I'm not sure I'm ready to settle down," he said. "I'm a catch."

I rolled my eyes—he was always going on about what a catch he was. I didn't have time to dissect his little tantrum and what it meant for Brickhouse's and his relationship because the patio door slid open.

Kevin stepped inside, paused a second as he looked at me, and said, "Hello, Nina. Fancy seeing you here."

The worst of the weather may have blown over, but by the look in Kevin's eyes, the real storm was just beginning.

I looked at Perry. "I'll take that refill now."

Chapter Three

It was a motley crew that followed Kevin inside.

A drenched motley crew, four of them in all, all as mismatched as the chairs Kevin directed them to sit in.

"Luvie, can I trouble you for a towel?" Delphine Reaux purred to Perry as she rubbed up against him. Whisking raindrops from her face, she batted her fake lashes.

It was last week when I started to wonder if Delphine was part cat since she couldn't seem to talk, walk, or stretch like a normal person. She had the sleek look of a feline, but there was a glint in her eye that warned she might be feral, so approach at your own risk.

I kept my distance.

"Absolutely!" Perry snapped to and dashed down the hallway, at her beck and call. Even though there wasn't a heterosexual bone in his body, Delphine had that effect on *all* men.

"A whole stack," I called after Perry. Delphine hadn't asked for towels for the others, who were more soaked through than she, because she'd been the only one to have an umbrella.

It spoke volumes about her character. Not that her character was ever in question. With Delphine, what one saw was what one got. Claws and all. And speaking of claws, her fingernails were painted blood red and bedazzled with crystals.

I had to admit, I kind of liked the crystals (don't tell my fashionista sister Maria). I could hardly remember the last time my raggedy nails had been painted. With my line of work, a manicure was a waste of money.

I was surprised Delphine didn't have the same problem, being in construction. But obviously she didn't get her hands dirty too often, with work, at least.

I stood off to the side along with Mr. Cabrera, who'd found the gin on the counter and poured himself another drink.

He was going to regret that decision in the morning.

Me? I was probably going to regret it in fifteen minutes when I had to walk him home and explain his condition to Mrs. Krauss. The man couldn't hold his liquor and was going to be falling-down drunk soon.

I'd known Brickhouse since I was fifteen years old. She scared me then, and she scared me now. We'd come a long way in our friendship, mostly because I'd discovered that she was more bark than bite, but every once in a while she still gnashed her teeth and took a chunk out of my hide. I feared that when I delivered an inebriated Mr. Cabrera home to her that this was one of those times when she would bite.

The group sat forlornly at the table, most of them dripping

rainwater onto the floor. I wasn't too worried about the old wooden boards—they were due to be pulled up and replaced any day now.

Well, it *had* been scheduled. I wasn't sure how Joey Miller's murder would fit into the renovation plans.

My gaze skipped from face to face. This group had all become familiar to me over the past week, yet in light of what had been found in the back yard, I was looking at them through fresh eyes. It was very possible one of them was a killer.

Delphine sat at the head of the table and to her right sat Brian "Bear" Broward, who only had eyes for her. He'd earned his nickname because he looked just like a giant bear. Over six feet tall, he had shaggy curly brown hair, big round brown eyes, a rounded belly and a slightly hunched back. But make no mistake, there was nothing cuddly about him. He was more grizzly than teddy.

Opposite Delphine sat Ethan Onderko. If he had a nickname it would probably be something like "Serial Killer." I'm kidding, kind of. Mid-twenties, he was tall and skinny with a bit of a James Dean look about him with gorgeous downturned eyes that were black and devoid of humanity. With his slicked-back hair he had "bad boy" attitude stamped all over him. He favored white tees and ripped jeans, drove an old pickup truck and smoked like a chimney. I wouldn't have been the least bit surprised if he pulled a switchblade from his pocket and carved his initials into the walnut table—right after he stabbed someone with its sharp tip. He was terrifying.

On Delphine's left, Plum Reaux tapped her modestly-manicured nails on the table and made puppy dog eyes at an oblivious Bear. Tall (almost as tall as Bear), she was heavyset with broad shoulders, triple Ds (at least), a modest waist, and wide hips. If one "supersized" Delphine, she would look a lot like Plum, which made all kinds of sense since they were sisters. She embraced her womanly hourglass figure by wearing a gold one-piece jumpsuit that was belted just under her enormous breasts. With her dark blue eyes and long chestnut hair, she was va-va-voom gorgeous—even soaking wet.

Seriously, the whole Reaux family was stunning.

Too bad about their criminal inclinations.

Speaking of which, I hadn't seen Jean-Claude since I pulled in the driveway. I snuck a peek out the front window to see that the cab of my truck was empty. Jean-Claude was long gone, and I could only imagine where he'd wandered off to.

Or why he'd been so fidgety when we pulled up and he saw the police. As far as I knew he wasn't involved in any recent dirty dealings.

Which didn't mean too much. He was a sneaky one, and often kept his extracurricular activities a secret.

Most of the time.

I had once uncovered his secret life as JC Rock, an exotic dancer. He still moonlighted down in the Blue Zone to earn extra money, but that wouldn't explain his current nervousness around the Freedom PD.

It was something to look into. Later.

Plum flicked her gaze toward me, and like Ethan, I didn't see much humanity in her eyes. There was a cold calculation within the blue depths that made me shiver. I wanted to wring Perry's neck for ever agreeing to hire this group. Although, I couldn't completely blame him. It had been Mario who hired them.

Not that he'd brought this on, of course. No one brought on a *murder*.

Well. Okay. Sometimes it was brought on. By scummy people like Joey Miller. And if you hired Joey Miller, then yeah, I suppose you brought it on.

So...technically all this was Mario's fault.

Perry came back and doled out luxurious bath towels to the group. Kevin declined taking one and instead walked over to me while the others dried off.

"I need to use the facilities," Mr. Cabrera announced loudly.

I pried his empty glass from his hands and set it in the sink. He toddled away, bumped into a wall, and kept on going.

Kevin didn't say anything, he just stood close by. So close that his body heat radiated toward me. Raindrops slid down his cheek and dripped off his chin. The moisture soaked into his blue button-down shirt, which was already drenched and clung to his arms and chest, molding to his muscles.

Not that I noticed or anything.

That was me. Nina Colette Oblivious Ceceri Quinn.

With a bit of effort, I forced myself to look away. His quietness was making me nervous. Usually he was quick with a quip or some sort of criticism of my involvement—yet again—with his murder cases.

I caught him looking at me out of the corner of his eye. "I had nothing to do with this," I whispered.

"I didn't say anything, Nina."

"You were thinking it."

"You don't know what I'm thinking."

"Yes, I do, and you're thinking that this is my fault. Or if not my fault, that somehow I brought this on. I'll have you know, this is all Mario's fault. He hired them, fully knowing the Reaux family reputation."

"No," he said darkly, "you don't know what I'm thinking. Or else you'd be covering up. Wet T-shirts become you."

I looked down, saw my nipples standing at attention and gasped. I practically tackled Perry to grab a towel.

The corner of Kevin's mouth quirked.

I frowned at Perry. "You could have told me."

"What?" he said innocently. "Wet T-shirts do become you."

"Uhn," Bear said.

He pried his eyes off Delphine long enough to give me the once over. I wasn't sure if he was agreeing or disagreeing. I really didn't want to know.

Jealousy flashed in Plum's eyes as she gave me a dirty look. *Oh please*, I wanted to say. As if I was competition with her triple Ds.

She should be more worried about her sister because it was obvious Delphine was the competition for Bear's affections.

Delphine, however, *was* oblivious as she studied her nails, or at least pretended to be.

Ethan glanced toward me, then away again, dismissing me with barely a blink. *Huh.* No need to be rude about it.

Mr. Cabrera came back from the bathroom, took a look at me huddling under the towel and said, "Someone finally tell her about the headlights?"

"I'm going home," I said.

Kevin grabbed my arm. "Not yet. I have questions, lots of questions. For all of you."

I eyed the gin but decided against drowning my embarrassment. Mr. Cabrera, however, had no such qualms and poured himself another drink.

All I could picture was Brickhouse's teeth. *Chomp, chomp.*

"If we could get this over with, Luvie," Delphine purred to Kevin, "I'd appreciate it. I have things to do today."

I bristled at her calling him "Luvie" even though she called everyone that. I had no reason to bristle. None whatsoever. But bristle I did.

"Ice, ice baby," Plum said loftily to her sister. "Your boy toy is dead and all you can think about is your manicure appointment?"

Talk about *meow*. Maybe Delphine wasn't the only one who had feline tendencies.

Delphine narrowed her eyes but didn't say anything. Fortunately, Kevin did. "Boy toy? Were you dating Joey Miller, Miss Reaux?"

"We went out a couple of times." Delphine adjusted her skirt. "He was single. I'm single. No big deal." Tipping her head, she said saucily, "And trust me when I say he wasn't worth killing over."

I noticed Bear clench his hands. This grizzly sure wasn't happy that Delphine had been seeing Joey.

Kevin walked around the table. "When did Joey go missing?"

"Two days ago," Perry said. "He went out for lunch Wednesday afternoon and never came back."

"Did you think that was strange?" Kevin asked. "That he'd just up and walk away?"

"From the job? Or from *me*?" Delphine purred.

I gagged a little bit.

Bear patted Delphine's hand. "No one would walk away from you, baby."

Plum outright rolled her eyes and said, "Joey has a history of walking off jobs—it's why he's been fired from previous employers more times than I can count. It was a risk taking him on with our company, but we were desperate for experienced help and willing to take a chance. It's not like we're unfamiliar with shady histories and we believe in second chances. It was more surprising that he left behind his paycheck—not my sister."

Delphine said, "Jealous much?"

31

"Slutty much?" Plum countered.

Kevin jumped in before a full-blown catfight erupted. "How long had he worked for you?"

"Two months or so," Plum said, eyeing Bear's hand, which hadn't budged from Delphine's arm.

"And how long were you dating him?" Kevin asked Delphine.

"About a month," Plum answered for her. She pointedly looked at Bear. "She has a thing for skinny little runts."

It was an apt description of Joey Miller. Skinny. Runt-y. She neglected to add slimy, which would have also fit.

Delphine glared. "It's not the size of the man, it's the size of his di—"

The end of her sentence was drowned out by a crack of thunder.

"Amen, sister." Perry took a big gulp from his glass.

Mr. Cabrera wiggled his eyebrows and said to her, "Do you like older men?"

Oh good God. "Maybe it's time for you to go home, Mr. Cabrera?"

Bear threw a menacing look at my neighbor. "Good idea."

"Oh, simmer down. I was just asking." Mr. Cabrera topped off his drink. He added, "I'm a catch."

"You would be," Delphine said with a flirty smile, "except I heard about your curse. I'm too young to die."

Mr. Cabrera pouted.

"I should take him home," I said to Kevin.

Kevin raked his hand over his face. "A few more questions. Who was working here the day Joey disappeared? Who saw him last?"

"We were all working," Ethan said, taking a pack of cigarettes from his pocket. He shook one out, brought it to his lips, and reached for his lighter.

Perry walked over and drew the cigarette from Ethan's lips and handed it back to him. "Uh-uh. Not in the house."

There was a collective inhale in the room as we waited for Ethan to stab Perry to death.

Perry seemed oblivious to the danger as Ethan's eyes narrowed into dark terrifying slits. From Perry's outstretched palm, Ethan took the cigarette and tucked it behind his ear. His eyes promised retribution.

"Coffee? Cocktails, anyone?" Perry asked, his hand resting on Ethan's shoulder. "I just made cookies."

I thought Perry was the bravest man I knew.

"This isn't social hour," Kevin said.

Perry made a face at him and came to stand next to me. I could practically feel his itch to do something more with my hair.

"Who saw him last?" Kevin asked again.

The corner of Plum's lips lifted. "I do believe it was Delphine. They'd been fighting."

We all looked at Delphine. Kevin said, "Is that true?"

"I wasn't the only one who got into it with him that day," she deflected. "Plum was put out that Joey called her plus-sized—"

"I hate that term," Plum cut in, apparently still seething.

"—and Ethan and Joey got into it about the sawdust…"

"He was a slob. I can't stand slobs," Ethan said, looking my way.

I really wanted to go home.

"Oh, oh!" Delphine sat up. "Joey also argued with Perry about the work in the bathroom."

"That's true," Perry said darkly, as though remembering the argument. "He was trying to put in ceramic when we paid for marble."

If they'd paid for marble but Joey was installing ceramic, where'd the money go? It had to be thousands of dollars in missing cash. Marble was not cheap.

"He apparently didn't realize that I could tell the difference." Perry scoffed. "Amateur."

Scammer was more like it. I didn't doubt for a moment that Joey had pocketed that money.

"He told me that the ceramic was what Mario and I had ordered. As if. I told him he'd picked the wrong man to con."

"Wait," Plum said, spearing Delphine with a sharp gaze. "Did you know about this?"

Delphine didn't seem fazed. "Perry told me."

"And?" Plum demanded. "What did you do about it? We

run an honest business, we can't be having our foreman cheating our clients."

"Well, I was going to confront Joey about it, but he went to lunch and...I didn't see him again."

I didn't miss the way she faltered on that sentence.

Neither did Kevin if the set of his jaw was any indication.

Delphine had just lied. About which part, though? Confronting him or not seeing him again?

"It doesn't matter much now, does it?" Delphine said. "The man is dead."

"But where's the money?" I asked, and tried not to cower when they all turned and stared at me. "I mean, if Perry and Mario paid for marble..."

"I'm looking into it," Delphine said with an edge to her voice.

Her tone told me all I needed to know—the money was gone.

Kevin took a deep breath, leveled his best cop-like stare at Delphine, and said, "You've told me why everyone else argued with Joey that day, but what were you arguing with him about, Miss Reaux?"

Plump lips pursed like she'd just sucked on a lemon. Obviously she'd been hoping Kevin had forgotten about that line of questioning.

However, she was saved from answering by wild knocking on the front door. It was followed by female cries of "Let me in! I just heard the news! Let me in!"

Kevin crossed the living room in three angry strides and threw open the front door. A young curvaceous blonde, maybe twenty-five at the oldest, stood on the doorstep sobbing. Big breasts spilled from a skin-tight mini dress, and bronzed legs appeared to go on for miles.

"Who're you?" he asked, sounding completely exasperated.

The woman fell into Kevin's arms and cried a river onto his chest.

I hated her instantly.

He looked back at us for help.

"Delphine?" Plum asked, smiling wide. "Do you want to answer the question of who she is?"

Grudgingly, Delphine said, "Her name is Honey."

I could tell Perry was assessing Honey's sky-high blond hair as he said, "Honey who?"

"Does she like older men?" Mr. Cabrera smiled and waggled his eyebrows at her.

"That's it," I said to him, taking his drink away. "I'm cutting you off."

The woman who clung to Kevin managed to control her crying long enough to peer up at him through glistening blue eyes. "I'm Honey Miller. Joey Miller's wife."

Chapter Four

"His wife?" I echoed. I gave Mr. Cabrera back his drink but only after taking a sip. This kind of bombshell called for it.

"I thought he was single?" Perry said.

"So did I!" Delphine pressed her palms to her chest emphatically as though the act of squishing her boobies so hard that they practically erupted from her shirt would prove her innocence.

It succeeded only in making Bear drool.

"Honey is who Delphine and Joey were fighting about the day he walked out," Plum tattled.

I noticed Bear removed his hand from Delphine's arm (but not his eyes from her chest). Plum noticed his withdrawal, too. She was trying hard to hide her smile.

Ethan still watched Perry like a hawk eyed its prey. I wished Perry had just let the man smoke.

Thunder cracked again, and I nearly jumped out of my skin as Ethan's gaze shifted to me.

"Can I go home now?" I asked Kevin.

"Where's Joey?" Honey cried, drowning out my plea.

She had a screechy voice and it shredded my already thinned nerves.

"I heard he was found." Watery eyes thick with false lashes looked around. "Where is he?"

"Out there." Mr. Cabrera pointed to the back yard. "He's the one in the body bag."

"Okay, really," I said, grabbing Mr. Cabrera's arm. I set his drink on the table. "We're going. Perry, call me later." I marched my drunken neighbor toward the front door only to be blocked by Kevin and Honey.

Honey finally pulled herself free from Kevin and stumbled toward the back door. She peered outside and gasped. As she started to sway Bear jumped up and grabbed hold of her. He cradled her in his arms and cooed that everything was going to be okay.

Maybe he was more teddy than I'd given him credit for.

"I'll get a cool cloth," Perry said, rushing off down the hallway.

Delphine folded her arms and gave Bear a jealous glare. "*Huh*, I see how it is."

"For chrissakes," Plum muttered.

Ethan shook his head, and said to Plum, "Maybe it's time to set your sights a bit higher."

"Like to you?" Plum snapped.

"Don't flatter yourself," Ethan replied coldly and then turned his attention to Honey's performance.

Delphine motioned to Honey. "Could she be more

dramatic? She didn't even like Joey."

"Says who?" Ethan asked.

"Joey," she bit back. "He said that even though they'd been married only three months that she was already giving him the cold shoulder."

Ethan rose out of his chair and went for the gin bottle. "Right. Because he's a pillar of truth and honesty."

"He cheated as a newlywed?" I knew he was a lowlife, but that was...lower than low.

Delphine shrugged. "If he couldn't get it at home..."

Bear continued to coo at Honey, who I noticed kept opening her eyes a fraction to see if anyone was paying attention to her in her prone state.

No one but Bear was.

I'd had enough. Besides, Mr. Cabrera was starting to look a bit greenish. "Don't you dare toss your cookies," I said to him.

He clamped a hand over his mouth.

"We're going now," I said to Kevin.

"What's stopping you from leaving?" he asked.

"You are. You're blocking the door." I tried pushing him to the side so I could access the handle, but he wouldn't budge. "Move."

"Aren't you forgetting something?" he asked.

I sighed. "Move, *please*?"

"I wasn't referring to your manners, but you do score points for politeness."

I sighed more heavily and debated kicking him in the shins. "What am I forgetting?"

"That's Perry's towel. Shouldn't you give it back?"

I hip-checked Kevin, pulled open the door and stormed out, dragging Mr. Cabrera behind me like a petulant child towing her rag doll. Kevin's chuckle followed us down the walkway.

My truck was blocked in the driveway by a police cruiser, so I left it behind as I headed for Mr. Cabrera's house across the street.

A verdant Mr. Cabrera took his hand off his mouth and said, "Maybe you ought to think about giving the old boy another chance, Nina."

At the end of the driveway, I stopped and looked at him. "And maybe you should just ask Brickhouse to marry you and get it over with, yes?"

He stared at me for a second, then bent over and tossed his cookies all over my work boots.

I took that as a no. A big no.

For both of us.

***

I left Mr. Cabrera with Brickhouse with no other explanation than "gin." Clucking angrily, she'd held open the screen door to him, and he'd scooted inside like a little boy who'd just been scolded by his mama.

I stomped through the wet grass separating our houses, toward my side door. Thunder rumbled softly somewhere far in the distance. Charcoal-gray clouds still hovered overhead but the rain had stopped and it felt like the danger was gone.

Well, most of it...

Across the street two men dressed in scrubs loaded a white body bag into the coroner's van. Another man stood off to the side, and I tried to place how I knew him. Easy on the eyes, he appeared to be older than me, maybe mid- to late-thirties, and was a bit under six feet tall, with dark brown hair and a strong chin. He wore a light-colored button down shirt, jeans, a black windbreaker with CORONER INVESTIGATOR written in bright yellow letters, and had a shiny badge clipped at his waist. There was a hint of mystery about him, but maybe that was my imagination running wild in light of the recent corpse.

As if realizing he was being watched he glanced over and faced me full-on, I *knew* I knew him. I just didn't know how. He studied me as much as I had done him, and I suddenly wished I didn't look like a half-drowned miscreant with puke on her shoes. Fortunately I had a firm grip on the towel wrapped around my chest or else he'd be getting quite an intimate look at me.

Giving me a curt nod, he turned his attention back to his work. Quickly I kicked off my boots and left them by the back door, hoping they'd disintegrate overnight.

The creaking side door opened into the utility room, which housed not only the washer and dryer, but most of my shoe collection and an assortment of cleaning supplies. As I headed for the kitchen, I suddenly realized I hadn't had to unlock the door to get inside. I knew I'd locked it that morning—I'd become rather OCD about the locks after one too many break-ins. Wary, I grabbed a hockey stick from next to the dryer and tiptoed into the kitchen, my weapon aimed high.

I noticed three things straight off. One was that someone had been rummaging through my cupboards and drawers. Another was the strong scent of Chanel perfume in the air. And the third was a tiny puddle of pee in the middle of the floor.

Letting out a sigh, I leaned the hockey stick against the island, grabbed a paper towel to wipe up the pee, and tried to get my adrenaline to stop pumping. After washing my hands, I strode into the living room, looking for my intruder and her accomplice. "Maria!"

My very pregnant sister appeared at the top of the stairs, a guilty flush darkening her full cheeks. "Nina! I didn't know you were home. Your truck is still across the street."

I folded my arms and tapped my foot as she carefully navigated the stairs. Each step was a hazard simply because she couldn't see her feet. Her enormous belly blocked the view of anything south of her navel.

"Don't look at me like that," she said, pouting.

She was a master pouter. Seriously, she could give lessons. However, I had spent my whole life building up immunity. "You promised me the last time I caught you breaking in that you weren't going to do it again. Plus, you're supposed to be on bed rest, remember? How did you even get here? And where's Gracie?"

Gracie was my sister's mostly blind, mostly incontinent Chihuahua. Lately, she'd also become mostly deaf. The only thing she had going for her was her innate cuteness—and my sister's adoration.

"Gracie's around here somewhere," Maria said. "Check under the couch."

In her pre-pregnant days Maria mostly resembled Grace Kelly. These days...she looked more like a relative of the Stay Puft Marshmallow Man.

Pregnancy hadn't been kind to her, or easy. A few months ago she swelled up and was diagnosed with a case of mild preeclampsia and prescribed bed rest. Her cheeks had puffed up and her ankles had puffed out. As she neared the end of her pregnancy, her bed rest orders had become stricter—the baby's lungs weren't quite mature yet and no one wanted a premature delivery.

At Christmastime she thought she was two months pregnant but a later ultrasound confirmed it to be closer to three. Her due date was in three weeks.

Maria's husband, Nate, and our mother had been taking turns caring for her. But my mother and father had just left on a long-planned cruise around Fiji so Nate had taken vacation time from his new job to stay home and look after Maria—who had a tendency to forget doctor's orders. She simply was not one to sit still for long and the bed rest was driving her crazy.

Therefore she drove everyone around her crazy as well.

I crouched down. Sure enough, Gracie was under the sofa, curled into a little ball snoozing away. Her "mostly" deaf might have become "totally" deaf over the last couple of months—she hadn't heard me come in at all. "She's there. Sleeping."

"She's been tired lately." There was wistfulness in her voice, an acknowledgement that her beloved pet probably wasn't going to live forever. However, I fully believed Gracie had a few more good years left in her.

Maria waddled toward the couch and slowly lowered herself down onto a cushion, expelling a long breath as she did so. Letting her head fall back onto a pillow, she said, "My doctor let me off bed rest now that the baby's lungs are mature. We set the date for the induction."

This was news. "You did? When is it?"

"A week from today, after Mom and Dad get home from their trip. I still have to take my blood pressure every few hours and email my doctor the results in case my blood pressure skyrockets, but the end is in sight. Thank God. Have you seen my cankles? Out of control."

Her ankles had long since blended in with her calves becoming cankles—and they were out of control. She hadn't been able to wear footwear other than flip-flops for two months now.

"That's still a little early...is the doctor sure the baby's okay to be delivered?"

"It's only two weeks early—and the doctor thinks it's best."

"She's seen your cankles, too?"

Maria chucked a pillow at me. I caught it and smiled. I tried not to tease her too much, but sometimes it slipped out. Payback for years of her torturing me about my looks. "And how did you get here?" She surely hadn't walked and her car wasn't out front.

"Nate dropped me off."

I'd taken to calling him Saint Nate for all he had to put up with. Maria had always been a self-centered and controlling dynamo, but her pregnancy hormones coupled with no physical activity had created quite the demanding diva.

"Why?" I asked.

"There was some sort of emergency at work. Something to do with the storm. He had to go in, and he didn't want to leave me alone."

Nate had recently taken a new job as TV news producer and loved it. However, it did make for odd hours, and when emergencies happened, he usually had to work, vacations or not.

"Riley called, by the way. He said to tell you he was fine and on his way home."

There was an ache in my chest that made me remember that his home was no longer *this* home. Even though he was my stepson, I loved him as my own, and hadn't quite adjusted to him living with Kevin full-time. He did stay with me every other weekend, but it didn't feel right. He belonged here.

Maria snapped her fingers at me, trying to get my attention. "Hello! My feet?"

I bit my tongue, rolled my eyes, and lifted Maria's feet, one at a time, onto the coffee table.

"Put this under them," she said, handing me a pillow.

I thought about putting it over her face, but then thought about the little innocent baby she was carrying and reconsidered. I lifted Maria's feet and placed the pillow beneath them.

"Water?" she asked.

Jaw tight, I headed for the kitchen. "When is Nate picking you up?"

"Tomorrow."

My hand froze on the refrigerator door. "What?"

"Tomorrow. He didn't know how long he'd have to work, so he suggested I spend the night here with you."

I bet he did. I mentally erased the saintly part of his nickname.

"I told him you wouldn't mind," she said. "You don't mind, right?"

I handed her a bottle of water and decided it was best if I didn't answer.

She handed the bottle right back. "It's not open."

I was about to give her a lecture on how a difficult pregnancy didn't give her the right to forfeit simple manners, but then I saw a flash of emotion cross her eyes and her fists clench.

Or try to clench, at least. Her fingers were so swollen it was hard for her to bend them. It was probably nearly impossible for her to open the water herself.

I twisted the cap off, handed the bottle to her, and said, "When was your last blood pressure reading?"

"About an hour ago."

"And?"

"The same. Nina?"

"Yeah?"

"Why do you smell like gin and vomit?"

"Long story," I said.

"Something that has to do with the coroner's van across the street?"

"Kind of." I filled her in on the discovery of Joey Miller's body.

"If I was dating Nate and found out he was already married, I'd probably bash him on the head and dump him in a hollow tree, too."

"Do you think Delphine is tall or strong enough to have gotten him into that tree?"

"Nina, never underestimate the strength of a woman deceived." Her eyelids drifted closed. "I'm tired."

"That's what happens when you wear yourself out snooping around my house."

"I wouldn't have to snoop if you'd just tell me."

"You didn't want to know, remember? You made me promise. And I never break my promises."

She'd broken in here at least once a month for the last four months in search of the ultrasound report revealing the gender of her baby. She'd made the doctor, a family friend, promise to not even write the gender in her file. Only on the piece of paper tucked into an envelope that she'd given to me for safekeeping.

"Since when do you listen to me? I changed my mind. I want to know."

"No you don't."

"Yes, I do." She frowned. "No, I don't. Yes, I do!"

I sat next to her. "What brought this on?"

With the past break-ins there had always been an instigating factor. The baby registry had sparked one break-in, the baby shower another.

"Nate wants to buy the baby a baseball glove."

"So?"

She wrinkled her nose. "Girls don't play baseball."

"No, they usually play softball, which also requires a glove."

"Not my daughter. She's going to be a girly girl. Pink dresses, tutus, piano lessons, tea parties, dance classes."

Her eyes turned glassy. She'd put a lot of thought into this.

"And if it's a boy?" I asked.

"It's not a boy. That's why I need to see those results. I

need to prove it to Nate before he goes off and buys my baby girl a basketball hoop or something."

"The horror."

"Are you mocking me?"

"Of course."

She pouted.

"What if it's a boy?" I asked again.

Letting out a deep breath, she said, "I don't know. I don't really like the whole sports thing. So sweaty."

"Have you seen yourself at Zumba?"

She glared at me. "Dancing sweat is different from sporty sweat."

"How so?"

"It just is."

I decided not to argue and instead pursued another tactic. "Nate was a pro baseball player. Peter ran cross country and also played basketball and tennis. They're pretty good role models."

Peter, our older brother, was a pediatrician who lived out of state. He'd just been home at New Year's and called every week to keep tabs on Maria.

"I guess," she said. "But I'm still having a girl. I refuse to have a boy."

Smiling, I hoped that she was having a boy. It would serve her right. But I didn't know what she was having, either. The results she searched for were locked in my Taken by Surprise office—still sealed because I didn't trust myself from blabbing.

I drew my feet up onto the sofa, unable to get comfortable, and realized something was bothering me. The mention of Peter had triggered another memory. One of him and one of his high school best friends running on weekends, teasing me as I followed alongside them on my bike.

Oh. My. God. It couldn't be.

I jumped up and peeked out the window.

"What?" Maria asked.

"There's a man out there who works for the coroner's office. I thought I knew him but couldn't place how. I think I just remembered..."

Maria levered herself off the couch and toddled over to the window. "Which one?"

"The guy over there, behind the van."

"The hottie in the windbreaker?"

Eyebrow raised, I glanced at her.

"What?" she said. "I'm pregnant, not comatose."

"Do you recognize him?" I asked.

She squinted. "He does look familiar."

I swallowed. "Does he look like Seth Thiessen?"

Her eyes flew open wide, then she squinted again. "Impossible," she whispered. "That's impossible."

It was.

Because Seth Thiessen was dead.

Chapter Five

"What kind of neighborhood do you live in?" Kevin asked as he strode in the front door several hours later. "I think the Mill accounts for the highest crime rate in the county."

"Have you ever heard of knocking?" I said from my spot on the couch. Even though it wasn't even close to being dark out yet, I'd already changed into my pajamas, was snuggled under a blanket, and had a bowl of popcorn balanced on my lap.

I was clearly not a party girl.

Gracie charged out from beneath the couch, her high-pitched barking drowning out the *Project Runway* episode Maria and I had been watching—one of many. There was a marathon airing and we couldn't pull ourselves away. Gracie barreled toward Kevin's feet, stopped abruptly when she neared him, piddled, and ran back under the couch.

"She doesn't like you," Maria said, stealing a piece of popcorn.

I smacked her hand—she'd already eaten her bowl. Tossing aside the blanket, I reluctantly stood, set my popcorn bowl out of Maria's reach, and went for the paper towels and spray cleaner.

"The feeling is mutual," he said, stepping over the new puddle.

Maria held out her hands to him. "Help me up. Gracie reminded me that I need to go pee."

"Charming," he said, but easily pulled her off the sofa.

"Hey," she snapped, "you try having an eight pound kid sitting on your bladder day and night, then we'll talk charming." She flipped him the finger, then penguin-waddled toward the powder room, cursing under her breath.

I jabbed a paper towel at him. "Do *not* get her riled up. It took me an hour to calm her down after one of her favorite contestants was *auf wiedersehen-ed* on an earlier episode. I had to ply her with warm chocolate chip cookies to bring her blood pressure back down—my last roll. So unless you want to either make a run to Kroger for me, or babysit her while I go, I suggest you play nice."

"With the rat, too?"

The rat being Gracie. I poked his arm. "Her, too."

He held his hands up in surrender. "Okay, okay. Ca—"

"And don't you dare tell me to calm down."

Pressing his lips closed, he pretended to zip them. There was a light in his green eyes, however, that told me he was on the verge of flat-out laughing.

"You're impossible," I said.

"Impossible to resist." He batted his lashes.

I crouched to clean up after Gracie. "What happened to the zipper?"

"It broke. Like that one time you and I... Ow! Why'd you pinch my leg?"

"Why are you here?" I asked.

"Are you seriously wearing your pajamas at six in the afternoon?" He followed me into the kitchen.

"Six is technically evening," I said, tossing soiled paper towels into the trash can. "And you didn't seriously just change the subject did you?"

Squinting, he said, "Are those flying cows on your pajamas?"

"Stop looking at me." I zipped past him, brushing so close to his chest that I could feel his body heat.

"No bra, either," he said. "You're just a girl gone wild."

I hurdled the back of the couch and pulled the blanket up to my chin. "What's that?" I said. "It's time for you to leave? So sad."

Smiling, he sank into the faux leather recliner. "No, no. I have a little more time before I go back to the station."

"Anything new with the case?"

He pulled the handle on the recliner, and the foot rest popped up. "God, I miss this chair."

It had been a little over a year since he moved out. A year of anger, hurt...forgiveness. We were in a strange place, him and me. Our divorce had been finalized months and months ago. But lately...it was starting to feel like a new beginning.

I didn't know if that was what I wanted.

His friendship was nice. But he wanted more. He'd never actually come out and said so, but I could tell by the way he'd drop by just to visit, the way he always offered to fix things around the house, the way he looked at me.

Oh, the way he looked at me.

I tugged the blanket up a little higher and wished I could pull it right over my head and pretend I didn't still have feelings for him.

Maria came out of the powder room, stopped in the kitchen for a snack (an apple), and then approached the couch like she was preparing for battle. I supposed she was—it was a two-minute process to get herself in a comfortable position. After a lot of moaning, groaning and cursing, she finally settled in.

Kevin stared aghast at her.

"Don't make me throw this apple at your head," she warned.

"I didn't say anything." He looked at me. "Did I say anything?"

"A picture is worth a thousand words," I said.

Maria gave him the Ceceri Evil Eye—which she was really good at, but he pointedly ignored her and said to me, "There's nothing new on the case you didn't already know. The scene is an absolute mess. If we find any evidence it'll be a miracle with the way it was raining today, and then having half the neighborhood traipsing through the yard."

"Speaking of the yard, when do you think it will be cleared?" The weather had already put me behind on my plans, and I needed to know how long the police would need the area cordoned off.

Kevin said, "A day or two. It depends on the coroner's report and if someone happens to confess overnight."

A chill went up my spine as I thought again of the coroner's investigator. "It doesn't seem like you have a lack of suspects."

He dragged a hand over his face. "That's true. I'm waiting for background checks on Delphine and her crew before I head back to the station for interviews. I have a feeling more than one rap sheet is going to pop up."

Undoubtedly.

He added, "Why did Perry and Mario hire Reaux Construction in the first place? It doesn't seem like their type of company."

"Caviar dreams," Maria said as she nibbled her apple to its core. She looked around—probably for my popcorn bowl. "Boxed-wine budget."

"When did the crew start working there?" Kevin asked.

"About two weeks ago," I answered.

"Was Joey Miller there every day?"

"Is this why you came over?" I asked. "To question me?"

He smiled. "It wasn't for the hospitality—or to see the rat."

"Hey!" Maria said. "You're going to hurt Gracie's feelings."

I was pretty sure Gracie was stone-cold deaf—her feelings were safe from his jibes.

Kevin leveled me with a hard stare. "You never had an argument with Joey, did you?"

"Nope, though I did kick him in the shins once after he grabbed my ass."

"Me, too," Maria said, holding her apple core with two fingers.

Kevin closed his eyes briefly, then opened them. "I can't say I blame him for trying. I mean, look at you two."

Maria glanced at me. "I like him again."

"But," Kevin continued, "after hearing the type of person he was, I am surprised that it's taken this long for someone to snuff him out."

"Well," I said, "apparently someone reached the end of his or her tolerance with him."

Kevin glanced at his watch. "I better go. I have some interviews to do." He stood and stretched. "Is it okay if Riley comes here tonight? I'll probably be pulling an all-nighter at the station."

"No problem." I was practically giddy at the thought. I missed that boy something fierce. "Hey," I said as Kevin strode to the door.

"Yeah?"

"Do you know the coroner's investigator who showed up today?"

"Which one?" he asked.

"The hottie," Maria said.

I frowned at her. "He's medium tall, dark hair, a little scruff..."

"Sounds like the new guy, Cain Monahan." He narrowed his eyes. "Why do you want to know?"

Cain Monahan. Not Seth Thiessen.

"No reason," I said.

"Are you interested in him?" Kevin asked. "As in *interested* in him?"

"Yes," Maria said. "Yes, she is. Can you set them up?"

"No, I'm not *interested* in him."

Kevin said, "Then why did Maria say..."

"She's messing with your head. It's what she does."

He glared at her.

"That'll teach you to call my dog a rat," she said loftily, then ruined her haughty moment by trying to stand up.

I gave her a helping hand and said, "The man reminded me of someone I used to know. I thought it might be him."

"Who?" Kevin asked.

"No one. A ghost."

Kevin opened his mouth, then snapped it closed again. He looked between Maria and me, shook his head, and pulled open the door.

"Oh Kev?" I said.

He looked over his shoulder.

I smiled. "Jealousy becomes you."

Chapter Six

A few hours later, my cousin Ana sailed through my front door, her long dark hair flying out behind her, and flung her hands into the air. "I'm gone for one afternoon at a lousy conference and you dig up a body across the street? You're a menace, Nina Quinn. No, you're a corpse whisperer, that's what you are. You're better than a bloodhound. Now," she said, plopping next to me on the couch, "tell me everything, including whether any of your employees had anything to do with it."

I muted the TV—I was still glued to the *Project Runway* marathon—and faced her head-on. "First, I didn't dig up Joey Miller's body. I wasn't even around when it was found. The storm blew over a tree, and the body fell out of the rotted trunk. Second, so help me if that nickname sticks, I know where you live. Third, I don't think any of my employees had anything to do with it. However, Jean-Claude did start acting strangely when he saw the police."

Because of her job, Ana had a vested interest in most of my employees' criminal statuses.

"Stranger than normal?" she asked.

"I think he walked home. He was supposed to get a ride from his cousin Plum, but he pulled a disappearing act after the body was found."

Ana gasped. "Walked?"

Even though Jean Claude wasn't afraid to get his hands dirty, he was inherently lazy. Walking a few miles home was definitely out of character. "In the rain."

"He willingly got his hair wet?"

"This is what I'm saying. It's strange."

"That's not good." She whistled low, then suddenly belted out a high-pitched scream. Scrambling, she flailed as she pulled her feet onto the couch and peered downward. "What the hell was that?"

"What? What?" I cried, pulling my feet up, too.

"Something licked my ankle!"

We cowered together as Gracie wobbled out from beneath the sofa and peered up at us with baleful dark eyes.

Ana pressed her hand to her large chest. "Sweet baby Jesus, I think I just had a heart attack."

I looked at her, then Gracie, and burst out laughing, falling backward onto the sofa cushions.

"Nina Colette Ceceri Quinn, it isn't funny!" Ana chastised. Then her lip quivered, and she started laughing too, collapsing on top of me.

I wiped tears from my eyes and bent down to pick up Gracie.

She climbed over my legs like she was scaling Mount Everest and lurched onto Ana's lap. She commenced in licking Ana's chin.

"She likes you," I said.

Ana patted the dog's head. "I think she just smells BeBe on me. I was just over there."

BeBe was Kit Pipe's massive mastiff. Once upon a time Kit and BeBe lived with me as boarders, but he'd since moved in across the street. Into Bobby's former house.

Bobby MacKenna and I had a history. Not a long one, but one that involved love, loss, and broken hearts. He moved to Texas at Christmastime to live near his ailing mother, and Kit had been house-sitting for him. But a few months ago Kit bought the house outright.

I glanced out the front windows at the bungalow directly across the street, at the glow in the windows. My heart clenched a little, like it did whenever I thought of Bobby. Truthfully, I'd been holding out hope that he'd eventually move back, that we'd pick up the pieces...then he sold the house to Kit.

The sale officially told me it was time to move on.

If only my heart would listen to that memo.

I tried to tell it that sometimes relationships just didn't work out. The timing was wrong. It wasn't destiny. To remember the good times and forget the bad.

My heart told me to shut the hell up.

"Nina? Are you okay?"

"Me? Fine."

Ana tipped her head, and her eyes softened. "You sure about that?"

She knew me too well.

"I'm fine. Really. How's Kit doing? He's been hiding out all afternoon."

She narrowed her eyes, but let her line of questioning go. "He's good. He just didn't want to get involved with the whole dead body thing, especially with the timing."

"Timing?"

"It's been six months since Daisy was killed."

Daisy had been Kit's ex-girlfriend, and for a while he was a suspect in her death. Ana had helped him through those initial dark days, but if anyone realized that the dark days never quite went away, it was me.

That was me. Nina Colette Corpse Whisperer Ceceri Quinn.

I was grateful when Ana changed the subject—she didn't like talking about Daisy any more than Kit or I did.

"Why is Gracie here?" she asked.

"Because Maria's staying the night."

"Maria's here?" Ana craned her neck as if she had missed seeing a very-pregnant woman in the room.

As if that were possible.

"She and Riley are at Kroger picking up a few things."

"Riley's here, too?"

"Kevin's working late, with the new case." I gestured across the street.

"Full house."

I nodded, not minding the company one bit. Living alone was proving to be challenging for me.

Maybe I needed to get a dog.

Gracie looked over her shoulder at me and sneered, one snaggle tooth catching on her lip.

Or a cat.

"Well...I have some news," Ana said, scooping up Gracie and cradling her like a baby.

Ana apparently had no qualms about being peed on. "What kind of news? Good or bad?" I watched the way she held Gracie and gasped. "You're not pregnant, are you? Oh my God, you're pregnant!"

"No, I'm not pregnant. But remember a couple of minutes ago when you said that you know where I live?"

I thought back, searching my brain.

She sighed. "When you threatened me about the nickname 'the corpse whisperer'?"

I snapped my fingers. "*Now* I remember. And seriously, I do know where you live. I will come after you."

Her big brown eyes grew round as her face lit. "I won't be living there anymore."

"What's that mean?"

"I'm moving in with Kit. This weekend."

My gaze zipped to her ring finger. Her bare ring finger.

"I know, I know. I said I'd wait until he proposed, but it's a good time. My lease is up, he lives right across the street from you—and let's face it, someone needs to look after you—and..."

"And what?" I asked.

Tears welled in her eyes. "I love him."

Reaching over, I pulled her into a hug. "I know you do, and he loves you. The ring is only a matter of time."

She sniffled. "It is, right? Only a matter of time?"

"Kit's not a stupid man," I said, holding her close. "Obviously, since he fell for you."

Kit wasn't stupid but he could be stubborn. I hoped he didn't wait too long to get that ring on her finger. Because she wouldn't wait forever. She was as proud as he was obstinate.

She swiped tears from her eyes. "Nina?"

"Yeah?"

"Can I borrow some clothes? Gracie just peed all over me."

***

Night had fallen early thanks to the stormy weather. Maria and I sat side-by-side in the dark, Riley occupied the recliner, and the only light came from the flat-screen TV above the fireplace. We were still glued to the TV for the *Project Runway* two-part finale (finally!), and Heidi was just about to announce the winner when voices arose outside and footsteps landed heavily on the front porch.

I didn't budge from my spot on the couch—I recognized the visitors' voices. They were friends, not foes. Most of the time.

There was a polite knock before the door swung open and Perry marched inside. Mario followed, nipping at his heels a lot like Gracie nipped at mine.

Mario was apparently in the midst of a long-winded lecture. "And what about the master bathroom? The pipe? It's not fixed, which means we don't have water. And the tile still needs grout, oh! And the washer and dryer hookup? Who's going to do that now? How am I supposed to wash my clothes? Never mind all the finish—"

"Make him stop!" Perry pleaded.

"—details. The painting, the trim work, the—"

Maria threw a piercing look over her shoulder. "Shh! Can't you see we're in the middle of something important here?"

They both immediately quieted. Maria had that effect on men.

Mario flicked a look at the TV. "Christian wins."

Riley groaned and stood up. "On that note, it's time for me to go." He headed for the side table by the door to get his car keys.

Maria let out a frustrated cry. "Way to ruin it, Mario!"

Dropping an overnight bag on the floor, he sat in the recliner Riley just vacated. "Do you want me to tell you about how my day was ruined?"

I eyed that bag.

Perry sandwiched himself in between Maria and me. "Oh, please do. Because we haven't heard enough about it yet."

Mario flipped him off.

"What's with the bag?" I asked.

"Kevin kicked us out," Perry said. "The police need to process the house to determine if Joey Miller got the old," he drew a line across his neck, "inside."

Mario said, "Let it be known that I didn't want to move to that house in the first place. It was Perry's idea."

"We know," Maria, Riley, Perry and I said in unison.

I was grateful that Gracie had slept straight through their arrival—Mario usually sent her into a tizzy. Probably because she didn't like nipping competition.

"Where will you stay?" I asked. "A hotel?"

"Kind of," Perry said. "It's more like a halfway house." He blinked at me.

"Something in your eye?" I asked.

"We're staying here," Mario said bluntly, his gorgeous black eyes daring me to say no to him.

"What?" They were joking, right? There was no more room at this inn.

"We're. Staying. Here." Mario folded his arms.

Maria put her hands on her hips and said, "Do you want me to kick his ass, Nina? Don't let this big belly fool you, Mario Gibbens. I can still take you down."

She could. And would. Which probably wouldn't be best for her blood pressure or the baby.

"It's not that big," Mario said.

Maria smiled at him, pleased with his statement, then shifted her gaze to me. "They can surely stay one night. Two, max."

"Where?" I asked. "You're sharing my bed, and Riley's home for the weekend."

"I can bunk on the couch," Riley said. "The guys can have my room."

Perry blinked at me again. "Please, Nina?"

"Fine," I said. "But try and stay out of Gracie's way."

Mario lifted his feet onto the chair. "She's here?"

I pointed under the couch.

"Maybe we should get a hotel," Mario said. "Do you remember what she did to my Gucci loafers?"

We all grimaced. His loafers hadn't stood a chance.

Mario was an interesting juxtaposition of a man. He loved the finer things in life like designer clothes and nice restaurants, but he was also cheaper than Brickhouse, and that was saying something.

Riley headed for the door.

"Where are you going?" I asked.

He rolled his eyes. At sixteen, he'd perfected the eye roll. "Out."

"Out where?"

"To a friend's."

"Which friend?" I asked.

He sighed. He'd mastered that, too. He'd obviously taken lessons from Maria.

"Well," I added, "you can either tell me, or you can stay here and take care of Maria for the rest of the night."

"Hey!" she said, struggling to stand up. "I don't need a babysitter." She tossed a look at Perry. "Can you give me a little help here?"

Riley had hit a growth spurt over the winter and was closing fast on Kevin's height at a little more than six feet tall. He looked a lot like his dad, with his dark hair, full mouth, and strong chin. His eyes, however, had come straight from his mom, who'd died when he was still a little boy.

He clenched his teeth and said, "I'm going to Layla's."

Maria, Perry, Mario and I said in perfect sing-song unison, "*Lay-la's?*"

With cheeks flushing a bright red, he choked out, "I'll be back at midnight." He slammed the door behind him.

"Layla?" Maria asked me as she absently rubbed her belly.

"First I've heard of her," I said, watching as Riley's headlights swept across the windows. I wondered if Kevin knew about her.

"She's a junior, five-ten, plays volleyball, has short blond hair and eyes as deep blue as a midnight sky," Perry said on a dramatic sigh.

We all stared at him.

"What?" he asked. "He talks. I listen."

"When does he talk? When do you listen?" I questioned.

"When I cut his hair," Perry said as if it was the most reasonable answer in the world.

I supposed it was. Perry was a master at weaseling information from his clients.

"We need to meet her..." Maria said as she wandered into the kitchen.

I didn't like the dreamy look in her eyes. She'd been cooped up a long time on bed rest. She was itching to throw a party. But I didn't think Riley would be so keen on the idea.

Mario said, "We have a bigger issue than Riley's new girlfriend."

"Joey's murder?" I asked.

His cheeks pinked up. "I was thinking about the state of our house, but I suppose that relates to the murder. Who's going to finish our house? And when? I certainly don't want to stay here long term."

I threw a panicked look at Perry. "I thought you said one night?"

He had the grace to look guilty. "Give or take a week or three."

"No," I said.

"But, Nina, the water line..." Perry said.

"Noooo." I stood up.

"The washer hookup," Mario pleaded.

I stuck my fingers in my ears and headed for the stairs. "I'm taking a bath and going to bed." Even though I knew I'd lie awake until Riley came in.

"Um, Nina?" Mario asked.

"What?"

"Don't use all the hot water, okay? I need to take a shower."

"What's that?" I asked. "You want me to sneak into your room tonight, steal your loafers and give them to Gracie to use as a wee wee pad?"

As if she actually heard her name, Gracie toddled out from beneath the sofa, growled low in her throat at Mario (who still had his feet on the chair), then went back into hiding.

Mario frowned. "I'll just shower in the morning."

"Good choice," I said. "Good choice."

Chapter Seven

Early the next morning, I left Maria in my canopy bed, threw on my robe and slippers, and scooped up a whimpering Gracie before she left a puddle on my bedroom floor.

The sun was barely creeping up over the horizon as I stealthily made my way downstairs, trying not to make too much noise.

There was just enough murky light coming in the front windows to see that Riley was tucked into a sleeping bag, sound asleep on the living room floor. I tossed a look at the sofa, wondering why he wasn't there, only to realize it was already occupied.

I edged closer. Surely he hadn't brought his new girlfriend home for a sleepover...

Peeking over the edge of the couch, I braced myself to see the face of the mysterious Layla and nearly jumped out of my slippers to find two brown eyes, hooded with thick unruly white eyebrows, staring up at me.

"Mornin', Miz Quinn," Mr. Cabrera whispered.

I blinked, rubbed my eyes, and looked again. He was still

there.

"I'd get up," he said, "but my head hurts too bad."

I had questions. So many questions. But first, Gracie. "I'll be right back."

"I'm not goin' anywhere," he said wistfully.

It was a warm morning, the humidity high. I set Gracie on the grass and took a moment just to breathe in the scent of spring. It was a special smell, one full of renewal and hope and...murder?

My gaze had skipped to the bright yellow crime scene tape across the street, which looked as unnatural in this landscape as a prickly pear cactus.

Gracie sniffed around while I stepped over my work boots (they hadn't disintegrated overnight) and walked the stone path toward the front of the house. Birds chirped loudly as I spotted Brickhouse's car parked in Mr. Cabrera's driveway.

If she was there, what was he doing here?

Or maybe that explained *why* he was sleeping on my sofa.

But would Brickhouse really kick Mr. Cabrera out of his own house?

I smiled. Yes, yes she would. Absolutely.

Across the street, all the emergency vehicles were long gone, leaving behind the bright tape and a sense of violation. I could just barely make out the fallen tree in the back yard and noted that it had been cut into sections—probably by the coroner's office.

I tried to imagine myself stuffing Joey Miller's body into

that tree hollow and realized that it wasn't impossible. Sure, it would be a struggle for someone my size—or Delphine's—but not too much for someone taller. Like Bear, Ethan, Plum. But with the hollow's opening a good three feet off the ground, whoever had killed him had to be strong enough to lift one hundred and fifty pounds of dead weight.

Dead weight.

I shuddered at the term, but it was accurate.

If Joey had been killed inside the house, someone had to drag or carry him to the tree, heft him up, and finagle him inside the trunk.

The more I thought about this, the more I realized that Joey's killer had to have put him in the tree at night. There's no way shoving a dead man into a tree during broad daylight would go unnoticed in this neighborhood.

But that didn't jibe with what I knew of Joey's disappearance. He'd walked off the job at lunchtime...

Gracie pressed her wet nose to my ankle, and looked up at me with eyes filled with cataracts. I lifted her up and let her lick my chin.

We had our good moments, Gracie and I.

Not often, mind you.

I turned to head back into the house when I caught sight of Brickhouse Krauss headed my way, marching across the lawn separating my house from Mr. Cabrera's like she was on a seek-and-destroy mission.

There was fire in her blue eyes as she said, "Ach! He's gone.

Gone! Snuck out like a thief in the night."

"He's on my couch."

Her eyes widened, then narrowed. She clucked loudly and mumbled something in German I was sure I didn't want translated. She did that a lot—clucked. Especially when she was angry...like she was right now. Steam practically spiraled from her ears.

She'd earned the nickname "Brickhouse" way back when I was in high school because, fittingly, she was shaped like a brick. From her short platinum blond spiky hair right down to her Fred Flintstone feet, she was a short rectangle. For a while, over Christmas, she had developed more of a pear shape when she'd lost weight due to pneumonia, but she was back to her normal size now that she was healthy.

"What did he do?" I asked. "Is this about the gin and tonics yesterday?"

I edged closer to the door to put myself between her and Mr. C. Anything to prevent another murder in the neighborhood.

"What happened? I'll tell you what happened."

She clucked so hard I thought for sure an egg was forthcoming.

"The liquor loosened his lips, that's what happened."

Uh-oh. This couldn't be good. Not after all his "I'm a catch" chatter yesterday.

"He came home going on and on about how he might not be ready for a commitment."

Gracie wiggled and I set her down again. She sniffed my work boots, tucked her tail and backed away slowly.

Ah, so she had some intelligence after all.

"He was really tipsy," I said, trying to make excuses for Mr. Cabrera. "I'm sure he didn't mean—"

"Ach! I'm not stupid, Nina Ceceri."

She usually called me by my maiden name—a throwback to my days as her student.

"I told him to sleep on the couch until he sobered up and that we'd discuss his concerns in the morning."

I could only imagine the tone in which she'd issued this proclamation to him. I was pretty sure I'd heard it back in high school after getting caught skipping class.

"When I woke up," she continued, "guess who was gone?"

"Oh."

"Indeed."

I fidgeted. "Do you want me to go get him?" If she were going to kill him, I'd rather it be outside. I'd never get the bloodstains out of the upholstery.

"No." She folded thick arms across her chest.

"Are you sure?"

"I'm sure I don't want to be dating a coward. Keep him here for another hour, okay? It'll give me time to pack my things."

"You're moving out?"

She gave a stiff nod.

There was a glossy sheen in her eyes that told me she had made up her mind. She wasn't one to show the softer side of her emotions, so it was obvious how this tiff—and Mr. Cabrera's midnight desertion—had affected her. "Do you need any help?"

"No. Thank you, but no."

"Okay." I shifted from foot to foot, nearly stepping on Gracie. "Then I guess I'll see you at work?"

"Is there work?"

She had a point. "Perry and Mario's job is postponed, obviously, so we're in a bit of limbo until our normal week starts on Monday."

Clucking again—this time more softly—she said, "I think it's time for me to take a vacation, on a cruise like your parents. They have the right idea, getting away."

A pair of robins cheeped from their perch in a maple tree. "They're having a blast." Well, my father was. My mother was still battling sea-sickness. Which was the height of karma after badgering my father to take her on a cruise for years. It had actually taken a bit of bribery on my part to finally get them on that boat.

"That settles it, then. I'm going to book a cruise," she said.

"A vacation sounds like a good idea."

"I'm glad you agree. I'll work it out with Tam. I'll be back in a week. No, two weeks."

"Wait—you're leaving right away?" Tam Oliver was my right-hand woman at work. She was my friend, my office manager, my go-to person when I needed any computer hacking done... She and Brickhouse shared office duties, though Tam had seniority and enough of a superiority complex to boss Brickhouse around.

"Ach. You were always a little dense, Nina Ceceri. What did you think I meant? Work is on hold. This is the perfect time to go."

With her frame of mind, I didn't want to point out that *work* wasn't on hold—Mario and Perry's job was on hold. Although this time of year was the worst for any of my employees to take a vacation, the look in her eyes softened my usual stance. I supposed I could spare her for a while. "Send me a postcard."

Lifting her chin pretentiously, she clucked softly. "If I have time. Don't hold your breath."

As she pivoted and marched back across the lawn, I felt an ache in my chest for what she was going through. Breakups were hard.

I knew from painful experience.

Pulling open the back door, I followed Gracie inside. The scent of freshly brewed coffee drew me into the kitchen, where I found Riley hovering over the Mr. Coffee machine breathing in the caffeinated steam.

He said, "It's almost done. I already gave Mr. C. two aspirin."

I patted his cheek and felt the stubble on his skin. He was growing up fast. "You're a good kid."

"I know."

"Modest, too."

"I get it from Dad."

"I know."

In the living room, Mr. Cabrera was still lying prone on the couch.

"You're probably wondering what I'm doing here," he said in a hoarse whisper.

"Nope. I ran into Brickhouse outside."

If possible, he paled even more. "Does she know I'm here?"

"Yep, and she isn't too happy about it. What possessed you to sneak out in the middle of the night?"

"She wanted to talk about weddings. Blech!" Then he suddenly burrowed into a blanket and threw a desperate look at me. "She's not in the kitchen, is she?"

"No, she's at your house, packing. She's moving out. I suggest you drag yourself over there and throw yourself at her mercy. Beg her forgiveness."

His bottom lip jutted out stubbornly. "Pah. She'll be back."

"Pah" was one of the terms my mother used all the time, and I wondered when he adopted it. "I'm not so sure this time."

He waved away my concerns. "She'll be back."

Riley brought me a mug of coffee. I loved that boy.

"By the way," he said, handing a mug to Mr. Cabrera as well, "Dad called while you were outside. He wanted to let you know that he made an arrest in the case."

I nearly choked on my coffee. "He did? Who?"

"Delphine Reaux."

Chapter Eight

I relocated myself to the front porch swing, along with my sketch pads and oil pastels. I might as well get some work done while I waited for the rest of the house to rise and shine.

Sunbeams sliced through the morning haze, making the dew sparkle and leaves glitter. There was storm cleanup to be done around my yard, mostly downed twigs and trash that had blown in—I'd put Riley to work later—but it was nothing compared to the damage across the street.

It was so like Kevin to call and drop a bombshell like Delphine being arrested and then provide no other details.

Had she confessed?

Had there been some sort of damning evidence found that I didn't know about?

I'd have to wait to find out, like everyone else.

Flipping open my sketch pad, I stared at the drawing I'd started months ago, the sketch of Mario and Perry's back yard once my crew was through with it.

Because neither of the men liked a lot of manual labor and didn't want to mow much grass, the design included a lot of hardscaping, in the form of flagstone pathways, a large patio with an outdoor fireplace, and a private sunbathing deck tucked into the corner of the yard. Along with a water feature and easy-care flowerbeds, the yard would provide the peace and tranquility the couple had hoped for by moving to the suburbs.

So far, they hadn't found much of either. Not with the renovations on the house and the body in the back yard.

Directly across the street, I spotted Ana's car in Kit's driveway and wondered when Operation Move-In would commence. Soon, I would imagine. When Ana set her mind to something there was no stopping her.

The screen door creaked open and a sleepy-eyed Perry tiptoed out, a mug of coffee in hand. I gathered up my supplies to make room for him to sit down. He looked quite preppy in his designer lounge pants and v-necked tee, but adorable with his bare feet, bed-head hair, and scruffy stubble. It was a rare moment to see Perry not completely put together, head to toe.

"Is Mario still asleep?" I asked.

He grunted.

"Are *you* still asleep?"

"I might be. This all feels like some kind of pot-induced dream." His eyes cut to me. "Not that I would know what that's like."

"I'm sure if you did, that it was medicinal."

He took a sip of coffee. "And yes, Mario's asleep. Last night he took one of those little pills your mother likes so much—she'd given him some after his meltdown about the hardwood floors needing to be replaced."

My mother had better stop doling out those little pills—I didn't want to see her in jail.

Well, okay, maybe jail for a *day*. But that's it. I swear. I'd even settle for one lowly mug shot.

"He'll be zonked out until noon unless a bulldozer comes along and scoops him out of bed." Perry battled a yawn (the yawn won). "How are you so peppy this time of the morning?"

I ignored the "peppy" remark, figuring that at seven a.m. anyone wide awake with a pulse would probably be considered peppy to him.

Setting my sketch book on the table next to the swing, I asked, "Did you hear the news about Delphine?"

"What news?"

I filled him in. He whistled low and looked decidedly relieved. "Delphine. Wow. Why? Because she found out Joey was married?"

"I don't know any of the hows or whys or whens."

"Are they sure it's her?" he asked, dropping his voice. He glanced around nervously.

Shifting, I angled to face him. "What's up with you?"

His Adam's apple bobbed. "Can you keep a secret?"

"Depends."

"Nina..."

"I can *try*."

Biting his lip, he searched my face. "Okay, but try *really* hard."

"You're making me crazy. Just tell me already!"

"Mario was the last one to see Joey alive."

I glanced around and whispered, "He was? When? Where?"

"Well, you know how Joey and I got into it the morning he walked off the job?"

"Over the marble tiles."

"Right. But there was a little more to it than that. He said some nasty things about the way Mario and I choose to live our lives. When I told Mario about it later that day, he went looking for a fight."

"Because of the nasty things he said or the cheap ceramic tiles?"

Perry's shoulders lifted in a shrug. "Not sure which was worse to him, but he was itching to go a round or two."

"Did he?"

"He tracked him down at his townhouse, and they had a little scuffle. A few punches thrown, a lot of yelling. But according to Mario, Joey was alive when he left. And he wasn't alone."

"No?"

"When he got there, Mario heard Joey arguing with a man when he knocked on the door, and then heard noises down the hall while he was inside. But he didn't see who it was. He said the voice was familiar but he couldn't quite place it."

"Arguing about what?"

"Something about a girl. Honey, maybe. Mario said that Joey was mocking someone fiercely for having feelings for 'her.' And said something like 'you love her, don't you?'"

"Wow," I said.

"I know. Did you see Honey? I don't think she's that much of a catch. Those eyelashes, sugar? She's trying much too hard."

"Maybe they were talking about Delphine." Bear certainly wasn't happy Delphine had been seeing Joey. But that didn't make sense—he'd been at work at Perry's house.

"Well," he said, sipping his coffee, "that I can understand. Delphine is a catch."

One I'd toss back. "What time was Mario at Joey's?"

Perry bobbed his head from side to side. "Two, three o'clock. He was home by three thirty. The crew was gone, so we locked the doors, split a bottle of wine and—"

I held up my hand. "I don't need the details."

He laughed. "We ate every bit of junk food in the house. Don't tell him I told you."

I laughed. "Promise." Then something he said registered and didn't make sense. "Why wasn't the crew there when he got back?" They still had a lot of work to do.

Rolling his eyes, he said, "Everyone came back from lunch in such a bad mood that I suggested to Delphine everyone just leave for the day. I needed a break. They're...a lot to handle."

With all the arguing that had gone on that day, I understood the bad moods. And that meant that Bear could have been the man Mario overheard talking to Joey.

Interesting.

"Well, Mario needs to tell the police about the fight and the person that was there."

Shaking his head, he said, "He refuses to talk. And now that Delphine has been arrested, he won't have to."

"Perry..."

"Nina, you promised you would keep a secret."

"I said I'd *try.*"

"Try really, really, really hard."

"I think that third really was a little gratuitous."

His eyes twinkled. "Really?"

I smiled. I couldn't help myself. Then I sobered. "Did you think that Mario had something to do with..." I gestured across the street.

"No. Not much." He held up two fingers an inch apart. "Maybe a little. Joey crossed a line, and it triggered something in Mario I'd never seen before. I was scared. For Mario and for Joey. But I guess I didn't have to be. Because Joey apparently had lots of enemies, including one seriously ticked-off girlfriend who did a lot of people a favor, in my opinion."

It was hard to argue with that. After all Joey was about the least likeable person I ever met.

I was ready for the whole seedy mess to go away and for

life to get back to normal. To forget about Joey and Delphine and...everything. It was time to look ahead.

A car door slammed and I spotted Brickhouse backing out of Mr. Cabrera's driveway. The back of her car was stuffed with stuff—clothes, boxes, a Crockpot. I waved as she drove past, but she didn't see me, or even glance over in a wistful goodbye to her former boyfriend. Sometimes looking ahead meant not looking behind you.

"That can't be good, her car packed like that," Perry said.

"No, it can't."

I wasn't convinced the situation between Brickhouse and Mr. Cabrera couldn't be fixed, but it was going to take more than a sly smile or a strudel this time.

"Breakfast?" I asked.

"What're you making?"

I laughed. "I thought you'd cook since, you know, you're living here free of charge for the foreseeable future."

He looked like he was about to argue, then said, "How about egg white omelets with goat cheese and bran toast?"

"Fine, I'll cook. Waffles with whipped cream and real maple syrup?"

"Sounds good."

We'd just headed for the door when the screeching of tires stopped us in our tracks. I turned in time to see a small sports car swerve into my driveway. The driver's door flew open and a wild-eyed man jumped out and raced up to the porch.

"Jean-Claude? What's wrong?" I hadn't seen him since

yesterday afternoon in the cab of my truck. "Are you okay? Where've you been?"

He waved away my questions. "You have to come with me, Nina. Hurry and change. No, we don't have time for that."

"I'm not going anywhere in my robe and slippers."

"Then hurry," he said.

"Where to?" Perry asked.

"The police station."

Ah, now I understood. "Is this about Delphine's arrest?" She was his cousin after all.

Jean-Claude dragged a hand through his hair. "Of course! The police are making a huge mistake. You have to stop them. They'll listen to you."

"Listen to me about what?" I asked.

"Delphine is innocent."

"Jean-Claude," I said softly.

"She's innocent, Nina. The Reauxs are lovers, not fighters. She didn't kill Joey Miller. And I can prove it."

Chapter Nine

It turned out there was no reason to go to the police station with Jean-Claude because he refused to tell me how he knew Delphine was innocent on grounds that he might incriminate himself.

That comment had certainly raised my eyebrows, but he insisted that *he* hadn't killed Joey, and that he didn't know who did, but only knew that Delphine was innocent. That I'd have to trust him.

Oddly, I did trust him—about this. Sure, he was a conman at heart but there was no mistaking his earnestness when he spoke about his cousin.

But unless he was willing to spill what he did know, then Delphine would be staying in jail.

Jean-Claude had left in a huff.

That had been two hours ago, and I was still stewing about it. I was feeling curious and anxious and a little bit guilty for not jumping in to help.

But there wasn't anything I could do unless he spoke up.

Nothing I could do except...

"You have that look," Ana said. She'd come over to see about borrowing my truck to haul her stuff to Kit's house and had stuck around for a cup of coffee.

"What look?" I asked.

"You're planning something."

I plunged my hands into soapy water. I'd never minded washing dishes—it was a soothing chore for me. "I was just thinking that if Jean-Claude doesn't spill what he knows then the only way to help him is to prove Delphine is innocent."

Ana's dark hair had been pulled back into a sleek ponytail. "And how do you plan on doing that?"

I wiped off the waffle iron. "I guess the only way is to find out who's really guilty."

She set her mug on the counter. "You mean, you're planning to catch yourself a killer."

I really wished she wouldn't put it that way. "I guess so. Want to help?"

"Hell, yes."

I smiled. "Good. You know I hate killer-catching on my own."

"The sad fact of that statement is that you've actually had experience with it. I guess it goes hand in hand with you being a corpse whisperer and all."

I threw a wet sponge at her as Mr. Cabrera dragged himself into the kitchen and lurched onto a stool. "Who's a corpse whisperer?" he asked in a monotone.

"Nina is," Ana said.

He winced at the pitch of Ana's voice. "I shoulda guessed that. It's her curse."

"What's with him?" she asked.

"Too many gin and tonics yesterday."

He groaned. "Don't say that word."

"Which one?" I asked. "Gin? Tonic? Gin and tonic?"

He blanched. "You're a cruel, cruel woman."

I slid another mug of coffee over to him. "I've been called worse."

"Make the room stop spinning," he begged.

"Put your head down on the countertop," Ana advised.

He smushed his face against the cool tiles. "Is Ursula back yet?"

"Nope," I said.

"She'll be back," he mumbled.

"Where'd she go?" Ana asked.

"A vacation," I said.

She glanced between Mr. Cabrera and me. "A regular vacation or one from him?"

"Both."

He started snoring.

We stared.

"Should we wake him?" Ana asked.

"Leave him." I motioned for her to follow me into the living room. For a house that was packed to its rafters with guests, it was relatively quiet.

Gracie was asleep beneath the couch, Riley was at work—he had a part-time job at the sports complex where my mean trainer Duke worked—and Mario and Perry had an appointment with their decorator. Maria had offered to go with them, and they'd taken pity on me and agreed.

I felt bad about it, until I could practically hear my mother's voice in my ear saying, "Gift horses, *cherié*, gift horses."

They were due back in another hour—just in time for Nate to swing by and pick up Maria.

As I gave the "Cliffs Notes" version of why Brickhouse had moved out, I handed Ana the keys to my truck, which was still parked across the street.

She headed for the door, jangling the keys. "It shouldn't take too long for me to move—I've been slowly taking stuff over to Kit's for months now. I'll let you know when I'm done so we can start our hunt."

"I'll do a little prelim work online while I wait for you. See what I can learn about Delphine and Joey."

She pulled open the door. "Don't go off without me."

"I'd never!"

She rolled her eyes. Then perked up when she spotted something on the porch. "What's that?"

"What's what?" I asked, coming up behind her.

"Looks like a present." She bent, picked it up, and flipped a small tag. "It's for Perry, but it doesn't say who it's from." She handed it over.

I shook the box. "Must be another gift from his secret admirer."

"I forgot he had himself an admirer! Who do you think it is?"

"I don't know, but whoever it is has impeccable taste. You should have seen the watch he got last week."

"It's a little strange," Ana said. "The gifts have been so expensive."

I glanced up at the sound of footsteps and spotted Kit coming up the driveway. "What's strange?" he asked, coming up the steps and dropping a kiss on Ana's lips.

Kit Pipe should be terrifying. He stood six-foot-five and didn't have an ounce of fat on his 250 pound tattooed frame. His bald head bore a skull tattoo, and his eyes were lined in black ink. Tattooed sleeves covered both arms. He looked every inch a Hell's Angel, but he was one of the best guys I knew.

"Perry got another gift," Ana said.

Kit frowned. "Here?"

"On the porch," I said.

"That is strange." He looked at Ana. "You ready?"

"Whoa-ho! What's strange? Why'd you say it that way?" I asked.

"It's bizarro that the admirer knew to leave the present here and not at Perry's house. Someone's watching him."

Ana shuddered. "It's beginning to sound more like a stalker than an admirer."

A shiver went down my spine, too. I hadn't thought of it that way.

"Mario's going to have a fit," Ana said.

It's true. He was. Mostly because he didn't have a stalker of his own.

"Maybe I'll hide it and give it to Perry later. Mario's already upset about the house renovations." I nudged Kit with my elbow. "Did you know they're staying here with me until their water situation is fixed?"

Stepping aside, he said, "I heard."

"That means they could possibly be staying with me for weeks, maybe months unless someone takes pity on my soul and fixes their bathroom." I stared at him.

Ana patted his arm and whispered, "I think she means you."

"No," he said.

"Please?" I begged. "It's only a matter of days before Mario is redecorating my house."

"It needs it," Kit said.

It was hard to argue with that. My room and the master bath had recently been done but the rest of the house could use a little TLC. "True, but he'll have Gucci wallpaper on the walls in no time." I glanced at Ana. "Does Gucci do wallpaper?"

She shrugged. "Maria's the one to ask about that."

"Anyway," I said, "you know what I mean."

"No," Kit said.

"You know," Ana said, "we do have that nice guest room. Mario and Perry could probably stay with us for a little while. We can swap weeks back and forth with Nina until their house is fixed. That way, it doesn't feel like such a burden on her."

Kit gave her a death stare. It was almost as good as the Ceceri Evil Eye, but not quite, which probably explained why she wasn't affected by the look at all. She'd built up immunity to evil eyes over the years, thanks to my mother glaring at her all the time.

She smiled fondly at him.

"Fine," he ground out, recognizing a losing battle when he saw one. "I'll do it." He turned and strode off.

Ana winked at me. "I'll see you later."

"I owe you."

"I know."

As she skipped to catch up to Kit, a sedan pulled up across the street.

A sedan that belonged to the coroner's office.

And if I didn't know better, I'd have sworn a ghost was driving.

Chapter Ten

I kept peeking out the window at the coroner's investigator—Cain Monahan—as he walked around Mario and Perry's yard.

The hair on the back of my neck refused to go down. He was a dead ringer for...well, a dead man.

"Who's he?" Mr. Cabrera asked, coming up behind me. He'd yet to go home, and I had the feeling he was dreading seeing the place after Brickhouse had packed up and moved out.

"He works for the coroner's office."

"What's he doing here? I thought there was an arrest?"

"Maybe the coroner found something in the autopsy that proves Delphine didn't kill Joey."

"Pah, she's guilty."

I lifted an eyebrow. "How do you know?"

"After what he did to her? Having a wife and all? Just makes sense. Plus, she's a little scary. I'm not convinced that her family doesn't have ties to the underworld, if you know what I'm saying."

I knew what he was saying. The Reauxs came from a long

line of criminals. How deep the felonious activity went, I
wasn't sure. Despite what Jean-Claude said, did it extend to
murder?

"Jean-Claude says his family is full of lovers not fighters."

Mr. Cabrera shrugged. "There's not a crime of passion
defense for nothing."

True. Once, right after I discovered Kevin had been
cheating on me with his partner, Ginger, I'd attacked him with
a hockey stick thinking he was an intruder. And when I
realized he wasn't, it had taken everything in me to stop hitting
him with that stick (after a few additional whacks for good
measure). Karma had bit Kevin in the backside big time when
it came to Ginger, and ultimately I had forgiven him. But for a
while, I'd wanted to kill him. Fortunately, I had enough sense
not to act on my emotions.

Mr. Cabrera nodded outside. "Maybe you should go over
there and feel him out."

"Why don't you go over there?" I was hesitant to see the
ghost face to face, and I couldn't quite put my finger on why.

Maybe it was because Seth Thiessen had been my first
crush, and I'd been devastated by his death.

His whole family—he, his mother, father, and younger
sister—had died when the small plane his father was piloting
exploded over a Kentucky horse ranch on the way to spring
break in Florida. Seth had been fifteen years old.

I suspected I didn't want to meet this investigator because
of his resemblance to Seth. I wasn't sure I could bear the

emotional fallout. "You're good at getting information out of people," I said, pressuring Mr. Cabrera. Because as much as I didn't want to be the one weaseling the info, I wanted to know if there had been a change in the case.

Mr. Cabrera held his stomach. "That's true. But I don't feel so good. Plus, you're prettier than I am. He'll be more likely to talk to you, especially if you fluff yourself up a bit."

"Fluff myself up a bit?"

"You know," he waved his hand. "Do your hair up, put on some mascara. You clean up good, Miz Quinn. When you clean up. Which, I might add, isn't often. You might have more dates if you did a little more fluff—"

I cut him off. "Maybe you should head home and go back to bed. Since you're not feeling so well."

He pouted. "Your couch is comfier than mine."

"Mr. Cabrera..."

"Uhn," he groaned and dashed for the bathroom.

I was beginning to think that he wasn't as sick as he was portraying himself to be. At this point, his hangover had become an avoidance technique.

Pulling aside the curtain, I peeked out again. The investigator was walking slowly around the yard as if looking for something.

Before I could change my mind, I slipped on my flip-flops, pulled open the door, and headed across the street.

My heart pounded the closer I drew to him, and my feet felt leaden, weighted to the ground.

I stumbled over a twig and his head snapped up as I bobbled for equilibrium.

The sun glinted off his sunglasses and I wished I could see his eyes as I approached. Seth had the most gorgeous brown eyes I'd ever seen. A dark chocolate with flecks of gold that always reminded me of Eastertime with chocolate bunnies packaged in gold foil. If I could only see this man's eyes, I could put my ghostly imaginations to rest.

"You okay?" he asked.

Heat flooded my neck, my cheeks. Lamely, I gestured to the ground. "Yeah. I tripped on a twig. Plus I have two left feet. The combination isn't pretty," I rambled.

He nodded.

I brushed the hair out of my eyes and couldn't help but study him like he was an amoeba under a microscope. The first thing my gaze settled on was the deep scarring that covered the right side of his neck, fading into the hair behind his ear.

To my untrained eye, it looked like a burn scar.

My stomach tightened. Seth Thiessen had died in a fiery plane crash.

The man's jaw was a little more square than Seth's, and he was a little taller. But those differences could be attributed to age. It had been almost twenty years since Seth died.

"Car accident," he said.

I snapped to. "What?"

"The scars. I was in a car accident. It's easier just to tell people than to have them stare."

I felt a stab of guilt. "Sorry."

He'd been in a car accident. Not a plane crash.

Seth was dead.

I was being crazy.

But...even his voice sounded like Seth's. "When?"

"When what?"

"When was the car accident?"

He didn't answer, and I really didn't need to see his eyes to know he was staring in disbelief.

I tried to play it off. I faked a coy smile even as my stomach churned. "I'm nosy."

"Who are you?"

His badge was clipped to the waistband of his dark jeans. It didn't have his name on it—only his job designation along with the state seal. I stuck out my hand. "Nina Quinn. I live across the street."

A smile twitched the corner of his lips.

A smile I recognized.

My knees went a little weak, and I shifted my weight to keep my balance. It was impossible. This man was *not* Seth.

"The infamous Nina Quinn. I'm Cain Monahan."

He took my hand, and I noticed that his hand had been burned as well. There was scarring on the top of his hand and his wrist—maybe higher but the rest of his arm was covered by the long sleeve of his light green button-down shirt.

The scarring didn't affect the warmth of his skin or the firm strength of his grip.

A very real grip.

Not a ghostly one.

Clearing my throat, I said, "Infamous?"

"I was warned about you."

I tucked my now-sweaty hand into my pocket and tried my best to wrap my head around this situation. People had doppelgangers. That's all Cain Monahan was. A doppelganger. "Warned? By whom?"

"A police detective. He said you'd probably try snooping into the case. That you fancy yourself some kind of Nancy Drew, and that I should steer clear of you."

"A detective? Tall? Dark hair? Green eyes?"

He nodded. "You know him?"

Kevin. The sneaky dog. "My ex-husband. And I don't fancy myself any kind of Nancy Drew. I'm a little too old for the likes of her, but yes," I admitted, "I've been involved in a few cases." He didn't need to know exactly how many.

The corpse whisperer.

I shuddered.

"Are you sure you're okay?" he asked. "You look a little pale."

I could see exactly how pale I was thanks to my reflection in his sunglasses. "I'm all right." I searched for a lie. Anything other than telling him that he looked and sounded and smiled exactly like a boy I used to love. "As much experience as I've had with it, murder is never easy to deal with. You must know that, with your line of work."

He turned a bit, toward the back yard where the tree had fallen. "Some cases are worse than others."

"How long have you been an investigator?"

He hesitated for a long second, and I thought he'd see right through my prying and not answer. I held my breath.

But finally he said, "About seven years."

"Did you go to college for it?"

He tipped his head. "My degree is in health sciences. I was a paramedic for a few years after graduation, and then this job opened up."

I rocked on my heels. "Oh? Where'd you go to college?"

He hesitated again. "University of Florida."

"Is that where you grew up? Florida?"

"Partly. Have you lived here, in Freedom, your whole life?"

"Born and raised."

"And how old are you?" he asked.

Suddenly, I realized he'd soundly taken over the investigation.

Before I could answer, a dark SUV pulled up. The window powered down, and Kevin stuck his head out. "You just can't help yourself, can you?"

I put my hand on my hip. "I haven't asked a thing about the case, have I?" I said to Cain. I hadn't asked because I'd been too busy grilling him about his personal life. I'd have gotten around to asking about Joey's murder eventually.

"Not a word," he said.

Kevin looked like he didn't believe us. He shut off the car and hopped out. "Good." He glanced at Cain. "Do you mind if I talk to her privately for a moment?"

"Not at all. Nice to meet you, Ms. Quinn."

"Same here," I said.

He took a kit out of his trunk and headed for the house.

As soon as he was out of earshot, Kevin said, "What was that?"

"What was what?"

"You and him?"

"I was wrong earlier. Jealousy *doesn't* become you."

He tipped his head back and sighed. "What were you two talking about?"

I batted my eyes and said dreamily, "Do you think he's married?"

Kevin growled. "I'm not jealous."

"Sure, sure." He wasn't fooling me.

"You really weren't asking him about the case?"

"No."

"Then what?"

"Stuff." I changed the subject. I didn't want to talk about Seth with him. "What brings you back here?"

He leaned against the hood of the SUV. "Jean-Claude said you had some information for me about the case."

"Jean-Claude..." I shook my head. "He says he can prove Delphine is innocent but won't say how he knows. He wanted me to convince you to let her go. He thinks I have pull with you."

His eyes darkened a bit and made me think I did have a little sway. I'd remember that.

"Family loyalty?" he asked.

"Maybe." I left out the part where Jean-Claude didn't want to incriminate himself by revealing his information. I'd work on getting his alibi before I turned him over to be questioned formally.

"Well, he's wasting his time," Kevin said.

"Why's that?"

"Delphine's case is all but wrapped up. Couldn't be prettier if it had a bow on it."

"What kind of evidence do you have?"

"When I questioned her last night, she admitted that she'd lied about not seeing Joey again after he went to lunch."

Aha! I knew she'd been lying yesterday.

"She said she was upset by what Perry had told her about the tiles and she called him to meet her."

No wonder she 'fessed up. Her call would have been easy to trace with Joey's cell phone records.

"They met up at his townhouse—"

My eyebrow shot up, and I wondered if she'd really met up with him to talk about Perry or for a little bit of afternoon nookie.

I shuddered at the thought.

"I know," he said with a knowing smirk. "Anyway, she said she met him there, says they discussed the tile situation, and that when she left he was alive."

"Did she say how he explained the tile situation?"

"A *misunderstanding.*"

"Were you *Luvie'd* to death?"

"Smothered."

"And the Honey situation? How did Joey explain to her that he'd been hiding a wife?"

"Supposedly he regretted getting married and that he planned to leave Honey."

"After three months?" I asked.

"Yeah, I'm not buying it either," he said.

"So, did she kill him during the meeting?"

If she had, how did he end up in the tree? "Did you find blood in his townhouse? And wouldn't killing him there mean it was premeditated? I mean, most people don't usually carry around hammers. Plus, if she'd killed him why not just tell everyone that she'd fired him and that's why he hadn't come back instead of perpetuating the story that he simply walked off the job?"

"Whoa, there!" He held up his hands. "We don't have all the answers yet. But we found her prints on the hammer used to kill him and blood matching Joey's blood type was found in her car and on some of her clothes."

He'd ignored my initial concerns, but his evidence was pretty damning. The prints were easily explained, of course, but the blood... "Did she confess?"

"Denies everything except her affair with him. She has no explanation as to how the blood got in her car and on her clothes and claims someone is trying to frame her."

Was it possible? Or simply the only defense she had? "And the townhouse? Did you find blood there?"

"Haven't found the crime scene yet. That's what he's doing here," Kevin said, motioning toward Cain's car. "We don't need the crime scene to prosecute her, but it would help. She had means, motive, and opportunity. This case is signed, sealed, and delivered."

"Did the coroner give you a time of death?" I was trying to nail down timeframes in my mind.

"Between three and five p.m. on Wednesday."

Perry's voice floated through my head, reminding me that Mario might have actually been the last one to see Joey alive. He'd been at the townhouse until three. Then there was also the mystery man Mario overheard arguing with Joey. I bit my cheek wondering if I should tell Kevin that bit. I didn't want to rat out a friend if I didn't have to.

Kevin absently looked into the back yard. "But we know he was alive at three forty-five. He answered a phone call from a pay phone around the corner from his house."

I let out a breath. That let Mario off the hook—he'd been

home with Perry by then.

"Who was on the phone? Do you know?"

"I'd bet my badge it was Joey's killer, luring him to his death. We're checking it out. The more nails in Delphine's coffin, the better."

"I'm still not convinced she did it. I mean, he probably had other enemies. Some who might have stopped by his place and argued with him, then lured him to his death. Delphine is easy to frame, especially because a lot of people knew she had argued with him about Honey. Plus, why else put Joey's body in the tree here? Maybe someone was trying to tie the death to Delphine's job site."

Dark eyebrows snapped downward. "Do you know something you want to share, Nina?"

Damn! He could always see right through me. "I just think you should look a little deeper into that angle." I peeled myself off the bumper. "That's all."

He clenched his jaw.

I smiled.

He clenched harder.

I shrugged. "I'm just saying."

"Well, stop."

"You're cranky." I gestured toward the house. "The back yard... When can I get to work? When can Mario and Perry get back to the renovations?"

"We'll know more in a few hours," he ground out. "I'll let you know."

"Fine," I said.

He was shaking his head as he walked into the house. I watched him go inside before I turned toward home. I hadn't taken two steps before I heard someone call my name.

"Hey, Ms. Quinn!"

I spun and found Cain Monahan jogging toward me. As he neared, he slipped his sunglasses back on.

Damn.

Kevin watched our every move from behind Mario and Perry's picture window.

I shaded my eyes against the sun. "Yeah?" I squeaked.

He stuck his hand into his pocket and pulled out a business card holder. He flicked it open, pulled out a card. "Just in case you have any more questions."

He gave a nod, turned, and went back into the house.

I wrapped my hand tightly around the card. I had a million questions, but I didn't know if he held the answers.

Kevin still stared.

For kicks, I blew him a kiss before I turned toward home.

Chapter Eleven

Mr. Cabrera waited for me on the front porch. Gracie wandered around, sniffing the bushes.

"Well?" he said. "What'd he say? Why's he over there?"

I lowered myself next to him. "He's checking the house and yard, trying to figure out exactly where Joey Miller was killed."

Mr. Cabrera whistled. "That'd be something, another murder happening in that house."

I wasn't worried. Mario and Perry had been home during the time frame Joey had been killed—locked in the house alone. And they would have heard or seen something if he'd been bludgeoned right outside their back door.

Next door at the haunted house, the neighborhood Realtor, Jennie Nix, pulled up with a couple in tow. They stepped out of the car, pointed at the crime scene tape across the street and got back into the car and drove away.

"That house'll never sell."

"Until I tell my parents buy it," I said.

His eyes widened. "You wouldn't!"

"I might." I really wouldn't, but he didn't need to know

that.

"This neighborhood has gone to—"

"Seed. Yes, I know. You've told me."

He grumbled but didn't say anything else.

Gracie hopped up the steps and nudged my leg with her nose. I rubbed her ears and glanced across the street. Cain passed by the window, and I couldn't believe how much he resembled Seth Thiessen.

I had to keep reminding myself that Seth was dead.

I'd gone to his funeral.

Letting out a breath, I realized that the key to putting the Cain situation behind me was to see his eyes. The eyes would tell me everything.

I glanced at the card in my hand. The coroner's office was located in the county's municipal building—the same place Ana worked. All I had to do was pop in to see her on Monday and take a little detour to Cain's office...

A loud truck rumbled down the street. My truck. I watched as it swerved into Kit's driveway. The bed of my Ford was loaded with furniture and full black trash bags. Ana honked and stuck her head out the window. "Give me an hour!"

Kit's Hummer pulled up at the curb, an armoire sticking out the back window, a plastic bag tied to a drawer pull blowing about. Kit was particular about his car, and I imagine it took some finagling on Ana's part to get him to use it as a moving van.

I smiled, feeling happy for them. They were pretty perfect

for each other.

"She sure has him wrapped around her finger, doesn't she?" Mr. Cabrera said, sounding disgusted.

"I don't think he minds all that much."

"On the surface, perhaps. But underneath he's probably mourning his freedom. The power to do what he wants, when he wants with no one to answer to but himself."

I gave him a sideways glance. "Or...he's happy to have someone to come home to every night, someone to share his problems with, someone to listen to his jokes, and who makes him laugh. Someone who loves every tattoo on his body, who smiles at him like there is no other man in the world, because to her there isn't. And he knows how lucky he is that she chose him. Just as she knows how lucky she is that he chose her."

Bushy white eyebrows shot up. "Pah. Next thing I know you're going to tell me that they'll live happily ever after."

"Maybe they will. It's been known to happen from time to time."

"Or they won't. And then the heartbreak will be worse when one of them leaves."

"Not everyone leaves."

His voice was hoarse as he said, "The good ones do."

I turned to face him. Suddenly his reluctance to get married made all kinds of sense. He'd loved his wife dearly, but she'd been gone a long time now. "But don't you think it's worth trying? Better to have loved and lost..."

"My head hurts. I'm going to go lie down."

"Forty-five minutes!" Ana yelled.

"What are you two doing anyway?" he asked as he stood up.

"Shopping," I lied.

"You might want to think about getting your nails done while you're out. Men like pretty nails, and you haven't had a date in a while."

"What happened to not believing in happily ever after?"

"I'm not talking about you gettin' married. I'm talking about how you're becoming a spinster. You gotta live a little." He did a little shimmy shake.

"Am I a catch?" I joked.

"Let's not go that far," he said. "After all, you're the corpse whisperer. A man's gotta have his head checked to get into a long-term relationship with you."

"Gee, thanks." I scooped up Gracie, gave Mr. Cabrera the Ceceri Evil Eye as I passed by him, and went inside. I headed straight upstairs and set Gracie on the make-shift doggy bed I'd made for her out of old towels.

As I turned on my laptop, I absently wondered where Maria, Perry, and Mario had gotten off to. I didn't think their meeting was supposed to last so long. On that same note, I wondered when Nate was going to swing by and pick up Maria. She was getting entirely too comfortable here.

Perry's mysterious package sat on my nightstand. I gave it another shake but couldn't tell what was inside.

I didn't want to think about him having a possible stalker, so I stared at the search engine I'd called up on my computer. I typed in Delphine's name and found a few pages of entries. Mostly reviews of her company—the majority of them surprisingly favorable. Plum had said they were an honest company, but I'd had my doubts simply because of their family history. I silently sent them an apology.

I searched for information on Joey Miller, but it was such a common name that I didn't find much of any use—there was too much to wade through. I didn't even know how old he was. I guesstimated mid-thirties, but I'd need his actual birth date or social security number to narrow a search.

I drummed my fingers on the edge of the computer and finally lost the battle within myself to search for what I really wanted to know.

I typed in Seth Thiessen + plane crash.

Unsurprisingly, there wasn't much information. The crash had been twenty years ago, after all. The best articles I found were from the *Cincinnati Enquirer*. Summed up, four people died in a private plane crash in northern Kentucky, shortly after liftoff from Lunken airfield. The FAA was investigating the deaths of the Thiessen family. Dad Eric, mom Annette, son Seth, and daughter Ashley.

Eric Thiessen had owned a German pub, The Black Fox, just north of here, and Annette had been the secretary at a suburban elementary school. Seth, a sophomore, had been a popular student at Freedom High School, and his younger sister Ashley, a freshman, was an All-State gymnast.

My heart clenched a bit at the memories. Of Mrs. Thiessen's smile. Of the way Seth always rubbed my head. Of my awe at how Ashley could tumble and do flips. I hadn't known Mr. Thiessen well—he'd always been busy working.

Leaning back on my pillows, I wished I could remember more from that time. But I'd been young and happily delusional about how suddenly life could change.

I gave myself a good shake and typed Joey's wife's name into the search engine. Fortunately, her name was unusual and there was only one Honey Miller listed in the Cincinnati area.

A few clicks led me to Honey's Twitter page. She had a lot to say about her retail job at a local mall and the colorful characters she met every day. Nothing about Joey at all. And she also used proper grammar, so I concluded she was educated—something I wouldn't have guessed by looking at her. I supposed that's what I got for judging people by their trampy covers.

It was obvious what Joey had seen in her, but what had she seen in him? He was at least ten years older than her, creepy, and a slimeball. Not exactly husband material.

I decided Honey was a good place for Ana and me to start our search into Joey's death.

Because Mr. Cabrera was right. Crimes of passion were common and it seemed to me that Honey Miller would have just as much motive to want Joey dead as Delphine.

Maybe more.

And framing her husband's mistress for the crime? Icing on the cake.

I also couldn't rule out the rest of Delphine's crew. All had beefs with Joey. All had the afternoon off from work. And I could picture all of them bashing Joey's head in.

I had a gruesome imagination.

I did quick searches for Plum, Bear, and Ethan and couldn't find much of anything. Depending on how Ana and I did today, I might have to get Tam involved. She was a computer whiz and could uncover all kinds of information with only a few clicks.

I heard a car door slam and voices rise in a heated cacophony.

Leaving a sleeping Gracie behind, I headed downstairs just as Maria waddled through the front door, Perry and Mario hot on her heels.

"You're impossible," Perry was saying.

"Me?" Mario countered. "You're the one who wants the gauche seven thousand dollar gilded mirror. It has golden lion heads on it. Lions! Hello, Liberace!"

Perry gasped. "That mirror is perfection. Maria, tell him."

"It is stunning," she said. "But perhaps not everyone's taste."

My sister, being tactful? What had they done to her?

"Liberace stunning," Mario said in a biting tone.

Perry folded his arms. "Admit it, the price tag is your true issue with it."

"What are you trying to say?" Mario asked with narrowed eyes.

Mr. Cabrera poked his head over the back of the couch. "I think he's saying you're cheap."

I threw him another evil eye. He was racking them up today.

He shrugged and lowered himself back down.

"Is that what you're saying?" Mario pressed Perry.

Perry said, "If the penny-pinching fits..."

Mario seethed. Steam practically shot out of his ears.

I couldn't blame him. He wasn't cheap, necessarily. He liked nice things. He was just more practical than Perry.

"I take it the meeting didn't go well," I said.

Maria lowered herself into the recliner. There was exhaustion in her eyes but also excitement, too. She loved being in the thick of things—something she'd missed out on while being on bed rest.

"That depends," Mario said. "If you enjoy a home decorated like a brothel then the meeting went perfectly."

"A high-class brothel," Perry clarified.

"I don't see why we need a decorator at all," Mario said.

"Cheap, cheap, cheap," Mr. Cabrera sang, and I wondered if he'd been drinking again.

"Impossible!" Perry shouted again.

"Boys, boys. You both just need to learn to compromise a bit," Maria said, sounding like the voice of reason. "Like Nate and I did."

Like Nate, she meant. As far as I knew she'd never compromised a day in her life.

"Speaking of," I said, "when is Nate getting here?"

Her blue gaze flicked to me. "Tomorrow. Monday at the latest."

"What?" I cried. Perhaps a little louder than I intended.

"Have some compassion, Nina," she said. "He's on assignment. There were tornadoes in northern Kentucky and he's down there helping with the cleanup."

"Yeah, Nina," Mr. Cabrera said.

I leaned over the couch and peered down at him. "What's that? You're ready to go home? Let me help you pack."

He pulled the covers over his head.

"That's what I thought."

Maria snapped her fingers at me. "Can you bring me a water?"

I sucked in a deep breath and headed for the fridge.

"If not for me and my frugality," Mario was saying, "we wouldn't have half the nice things we do. We wouldn't have a house!"

"And if not for your cheapness, then I'd have *all* the nice things I want."

I handed Maria a water bottle and noticed how Mario had fallen silent. I didn't blame him—Perry had hit a little below the belt with that comment.

Mr. Cabrera tugged the blanket off his face. "Nina, don't forget to give Perry the present that came for him."

I groaned inwardly. I hadn't warned Mr. Cabrera not to say anything about it.

"Another one?" Mario asked.

Perry rubbed his hands together. "Where is it?"

"My room," I said reluctantly.

Perry took the stairs two at a time, and I glared at Mr. Cabrera. He disappeared under his covers again.

"What's this about presents?" Maria asked.

No one answered her.

"Helloooo?" she said.

I gave her the evil eye, too.

"Hmmph," she said, clamping her lips together.

Perry was back in a flash and already unwrapping the present as he walked. "A Hermés tie! Ooh la la!"

Mario huffed, stormed past Perry and me, and stomped up the stairs. The door to Riley's door slammed and suddenly Gracie's barking filled the air.

"You should probably take her out, Nina," Maria said.

I clenched my fists.

"You're so gorgeous," Perry cooed to his tie.

I looked between them all, feeling my frustration rising. "You," I pointed at Maria, "can learn to say please and thank you." I spun on Perry. "And you are acting a little spoiled. Material things aren't what's important in life, which you'll soon learn on your own if you keep this up. Go upstairs and fix this with Mario right now. And you," I said, yanking off Mr. Cabrera's blanket, "need to get off my couch and get it through your thick bed-head that you're about to lose Ursula for good. And you can either be miserable and mourn her now or be with her for the next God-knows-how-many years – because you know she'll outlive all of us – and be happy as drunken clams together. Fix. It. And don't dilly-dally."

They all stared at me.

Finally, Perry said, "Drunken clams?"

"Argh!" Jamming my feet into my flip-flops, I grabbed my purse and walked out the front door.

Chapter Twelve

Ana handed me a Twizzler. "So you just left them all there?"

We sat in Ana's hatchback in a parking lot across the street from Joey Miller's townhouse, an end unit in a small complex, discussing my earlier outburst toward my house guests. "I couldn't take another second of them."

This wasn't Ana's and my first stakeout.

Or second.

We'd come prepared with Twizzlers, Snickers bars, chips, and Dr Pepper. Fortunately the surveillance of Honey Miller included restrooms with the close proximity of an UDF—a gas station convenience store that anchored the strip mall where we were parked—and where we bought our goodies. I couldn't help but remember our first stakeout and how Ana had to pee in the woods. It hadn't been pretty with the discovery of poison ivy nearby. Amusing, yes. Pretty, no.

"They worked my last nerve," I said.

"How much of it was their behavior versus your mixed-up feelings about that guy Cain?"

I'd told her all about the mysterious Cain Monahan. She'd

never known Seth—she had moved to Freedom after he died, but she knew my heartbreak over his death.

"Maybe some," I admitted.

"Maybe a lot."

I chewed on my licorice. Duke, my trainer, would have a stroke if he knew all the junk I'd eaten today. With any luck he'd never, ever, find out.

Across the street no one had gone in or out of the Miller's townhouse. Two cars sat in a narrow driveway, a pickup that belonged to Joey and a sporty white Mazda that Honey drove.

We knew Honey was home because we'd seen her walk by the front window several times, a cell phone glued to her ear.

She'd been laughing as she talked.

Not quite the behavior of a grieving widow.

"What are you going to do about this Cain situation?" Ana asked. "I can see how much it's bugging you."

Sunbeams bounced off the windshield, highlighting all the rain spots and streaks left behind by yesterday's storm. "I need to see his eyes. Then I'll know for sure that Cain isn't Seth, and I'll be able to put this whole thing to rest."

"You don't really think this guy is Seth, do you?"

My mind said no.

My heart said maybe.

I answered as honestly as I could. "I don't know."

"Well, whatever you're planning to get to the bottom of this, I'm in."

"What would I do without you?"

"Your life would be *soooo* boring." She grinned at me, and then wrestled another Twizzler from the package.

A car pulled into the lot and parked next to us. A young woman glanced over and gave me a suspicious stare.

That was me. Nina Colette Suspicious Ceceri Quinn.

I offered her a smile to prove that I wasn't some crazy whack-job lurking in a parking lot, but it apparently only confirmed her suspicions. She backed out of her spot and parked in the next row over.

"Are we going to go and talk to Honey?" Ana asked.

I stretched my legs, grateful for the extra room on the passenger side. "In a little bit. I just want to watch her for a while. See if anyone comes or goes."

The parking lot we were in served a strip mall of five businesses, with the UDF on one end and a bank on the other. In between were a pizzeria, a dance studio, and a dry cleaner. I looked over my shoulder at the bank, then at the convenience store.

"What are you looking at?" Ana asked.

"The businesses here are bound to have surveillance cameras, especially the bank and the convenience store."

Her brown eyes widened. "You think they might have recorded something across the street?"

I knew from Perry that Mario had last seen Joey at three o'clock and that he hadn't been alone. Had the cameras caught the identity of the mystery man who'd been arguing with Joey?

I said, "I'm just wondering if Joey was seen going out after Delphine left the other day."

Or after Mario left...

"Or if he let his killer in," Ana said. "How can we get our hands on the surveillance tapes?"

Good question. The bank certainly wasn't going to hand over their footage without a warrant.

The convenience store, however, might be convinced to let me view it if I came up with a whopper of a lie. I ran my idea by her. "What if we tell the manager that my car was a victim of a hit and run on Wednesday? But tell him I'm not sure where it happened and thought it might have been in this parking lot, blah, blah, blah. I'll ask to look at his tapes to see if the accident had happened here."

"You're a genius. An evil genius."

The nickname was supremely better than "corpse whisperer."

"Let's go in and give it a go," I said.

Ana groaned. "Uh, not so fast."

"Why not?"

She nodded next to her. "He's why not."

In my excitement about my plan, I'd neglected to notice the SUV that had pulled in next to Ana's side of the car.

The one with Kevin at the wheel.

He gave me a finger wave.

"Shit," I mumbled.

"Exactly what I was thinking," Ana said.

Clouds crowded out the sun as Kevin got out and tapped on Ana's window. She lowered it. He leaned in. "The dispatcher forwarded me a report of two suspicious women sitting in the UDF's parking lot."

Darlene, the weekend dispatcher, knew Ana and me well.

"We're hardly suspicious," Ana said. "Just sitting here eating our Twizzlers and drinking our Dr Peppers."

His eyes narrowed. "Why are you sitting here at all, as if I didn't already know?"

I plastered on my sincerest fake smile. "Have you been to my house today? It's crazy town. I needed to escape for a bit."

He said, "Your whole life is crazy town, Nina."

There was no arguing with that.

"But," he added, "you just happened to escape to the parking lot across the street from Joey Miller's townhouse?"

My eyes widened dramatically. "It is?"

But even as I said it, Honey Miller stepped out her front door decked out in a micro mini, sequined tank top, and five-inch stilettos.

She was on the move.

Ana said, "We should probably head home now. I have all that unpacking to do."

She'd seen Honey, too, and was trying to get us out of there so we could follow her.

"Good idea," I said enthusiastically.

"Yes," Kevin deadpanned. "A good idea."

Since my plan had been thwarted by his arrival, I thought it was probably wise to let him in on my idea. "By the way, Kev, did you notice the surveillance cameras on these buildings? They might have picked up something on the day Joey died."

His jaw clenched. He was bound to have quite the aching jaw tonight.

"The tapes are already being reviewed, Nina. I told you to stay out of it."

"Fine, fine," I said. "We're leaving."

He backed up a step. "I'll follow you home to make sure you get there safely."

"That's sweet of you," I said dryly.

"I'm a nice guy like that." He hopped back into his car.

Ana powered up the window and said, "Great, now what? Honey's backing out right now."

I glanced between Honey's car and Kevin's angry expression.

He was about to get really furious at me.

"We go with Honey," I said. "Kevin will just have to tag along."

Ana rubbed her hands together. "This is the second most exciting thing to happen to me this week." Pulling out of the parking lot, she followed Honey as she headed south.

"What was the first? Moving in with Kit?"

Her eyes flared and she blushed to the roots of her hair.

"Well, it was *something* to do with Kit."

"My fault for asking."

"Don't get snippy with me just because you're turning into a spinster."

"You've been talking to Mr. Cabrera."

"We *are* neighbors now."

"I'm not a spinster. Who even uses that word any more?"

"What would you call it?" she asked. "When you haven't been with anyone in five months—"

Technically six. Not that I was counting.

"—and refuse to even date? You're not getting any younger. You don't want to dry out and become an old prune, do you?" Puckering her lips, she sucked in her cheeks, and made an ungodly slurping noise.

Ahead, Honey used her blinker before turning right. She obeyed all traffic laws and drove cautiously. "I'd call it selective. And no woman *needs* a man. I'm perfectly happy being single."

Ana rolled her eyes. "I know women don't need men to be happy, but you've cut them off completely."

She was right—I had cut myself off from dating. Afraid to be hurt again.

With a sudden start, I realized I'd turned into Mr. Cabrera. Mr. Cabrera!

Sure, our situations were different, but our motives were the same.

"I need a date," I said in a panic.

"I know, this is what I've been saying."

"Fix me up! Anyone! Well, maybe not one of your probationers. And you know I like taller guys. Oh, and his teeth..."

"Nina."

"What?"

"Beggars and choosers."

I stuck my tongue out at her.

"There is someone I have in mind," she said, slowing at a four-way stop sign.

"Who?"

"He's driving behind us."

I peeked in the visor's vanity mirror. Kevin was fidgeting in his seat. "Kevin?"

"Why not?"

"Why?" I countered.

"He loves you."

Maybe. Maybe not. "I don't know about dating him."

"You always say how you believe in second chances, remember?"

Damn, I hated when she threw my words back at me. "I remember."

"Then it's settled!"

"No!"

"Spinster," she said.

"I'll think about it."

"Don't think too long." She made a pruny face again.

Honey turned left ahead of us, onto a road that led even farther away from my house. As soon as Ana followed her, my cell phone rang.

I didn't even need to look at the readout to see who was calling. I answered on the second ring. "I don't believe you used your blinker at that last turn, Detective Quinn. You can be cited for that."

"Where are you two going?"

"Home?"

"It's in the other direction, Nina."

"We're taking the scenic route."

Ana nodded. "That's right. The scenic route."

"You wouldn't be following Honey Miller, would you?"

"I don't know what you mean."

"Go home, Nina."

I made crackly noises. "What? I can't hear you. There's too much static on the line."

Ana followed Honey into a popular park. The place was packed with people enjoying the day, though I thought their delight would be coming to an end soon if the clouds on the horizon were any indication. They were coming in fast, and there was electricity in the air, a warning for people to take cover.

Honey pulled into a parking spot, and Ana parked a row behind her. Kevin pulled in next to us. He jumped out of his truck, pulled open Ana's back door, and slid inside.

"Twizzler?" I offered him.

"I really don't want to arrest the two of you, but I will if I have to."

"What are we doing?" I asked. "We're just driving."

"You're interfering in my case. And unsurprisingly, I received a call from the station a minute ago letting me know that Joey received another visitor besides Delphine late Wednesday afternoon."

"Snickers?" I asked.

Ana glanced at me. "You knew that? I can see you keeping something from him, but not me!"

"I...uh..."

"Nina Quinn," Ana cried. "You best explain yourself."

"Yes," Kevin said. "Please do."

She flashed him a stay-out-of-it look.

Holding my hands up in surrender, I said, "I made a promise to Perry."

"Promise or no," Kevin said, "you had a duty to tell me."

"And me!" Ana said.

"Fine. Then I guess I should tell you that Mario said Joey wasn't alone in his house. That Joey'd been arguing with another man when he got there."

Ana said, "You're forgiven. Who was the guy?"

"He didn't know." I told them what Mario had overheard. "And we know Mario had nothing to do with Joey's death because of that call he got, right, Kevin? And Perry is Mario's alibi for the rest of the time. So, really, no harm no foul."

"Nina," Kevin said through clenched teeth.

Uh-oh.

Looking around for an escape, I found one in Honey exiting her car. "She's getting out!" I quickly made a run for it before Kevin could slap a pair of cuffs on me. Keeping a safe distance, I speed-walked, tailing Honey as she made her way down a busy pathway that twined around a lake.

It didn't take but a few minutes for Kevin and Ana to catch up to me, which spoke volumes about my fitness level. I really needed to see Duke more often.

Kevin said, "We're not done with our conversation."

"Fine," I said, "but could we at least put it on hold for a few minutes? Honey is clearly planning to meet someone here, and I'd like to know who it is."

"You can't possibly know why she's here," he said in a condescending tone that made me bristle.

This. This was why I couldn't date him.

"Please." Ana wedged herself in between the two of us. "She's definitely planning a hook-up."

When Honey suddenly stopped at a scenic spot overlooking the lake, the three of us dropped onto a bench, keeping her in view but not getting too close. She didn't seem to have a clue that she was being followed.

"How do you know?" he asked.

"Look at her shoes," Ana said. "She's dressed to meet a

man."

I nodded. "No woman in her right mind wears five-inch hooker heels to the park for a spring stroll."

"You two have lost your minds."

"Never underestimate the power of women's intuition," I said.

"Or our ability to pick up on hoochie vibes," Ana added.

Kevin raked a hand down his face. "I don't have time for this."

"Look!" Ana said. "She's waving at someone coming down the hill."

Who would it be? The person Mario overheard arguing with Joey? *You love her, don't you?*

We all leaned forward, looking anything but inconspicuous. "Do you see who it is?" I asked.

"Not yet," Ana said.

"There!" Kevin said excitedly.

I stole a look at him. He shrugged. "When in Rome..."

We watched as a man raced into Honey's open arms.

Watched as they kissed passionately.

"Is that..." Kevin rubbed his eyes.

"Yes," Ana said. "Yes, it is."

Both of them looked at me. I couldn't say anything at all. It was suddenly very clear why Jean-Claude was afraid to incriminate himself.

He was having an affair with Honey Miller.

Chapter Thirteen

Kevin lurched off the bench and stormed toward the lovebirds.

"Where's he going?" I asked Ana, hearing the distress in my own voice.

"To confront them, I guess." She grabbed my arm and tugged. "Come on, I want to hear this."

"Doesn't he need backup or something?"

Ana pulled me along. "Jean-Claude is a lover, not a fighter, remember?"

"I was more worried about Honey going after Kevin."

"Those shoes could definitely be used as a dangerous weapon, but those are Louboutins. No way is she getting blood on them. Kevin will be fine."

"I meant that she'd start groping him. It wouldn't be the first time."

Ana's eyebrows shot up. "He is single..."

"Yes he is," I snapped. I just didn't know if I could go down that path again.

"Spinster," she whispered as we crept up behind Kevin,

who stood at the edge of the overlook platform, seemingly to wait for a break in the action before he barged in on the rendezvous.

Jean-Claude and Honey were happily oblivious to the approaching storm as they mauled each other. A mother walking past covered her young son's eyes and shot the lovey-dovey duo an angry stare.

"I'm starting to feel queasy," I whispered.

"Are they even breathing?" Ana asked.

Kevin glanced over his shoulder at us. "You two should go back to the car."

We shook our heads and stayed put.

He should have called for police backup—he was outnumbered by us. Apparently realizing that arguing with us was pointless, he took a step toward the couple and cleared his throat loudly.

"The slurping noise," Ana said, clapping her hands over her ears. "I can't take it!"

I hadn't been kidding about feeling queasy. Between the slurping and Jean-Claude's tongue practically bathing Honey's face, I'd seen more than enough.

"Jean-Claude Reaux!" I shouted in my best angry stepmother tone. It was rusty—I hadn't had to use it on Riley in a while—but it did the job. Jean-Claude jumped back, a guilty flush creeping up his neck.

Honey blinked, momentarily stunned by the loss of Jean-Claude's tongue. Then clarity came into her eyes as she took in the surroundings. Me, jabbing Jean-Claude with my index finger. Kevin, wearing his crankiest cop look. Ana, looking like she wanted to hurl.

Honey's hand went to her mouth, and her eyes widened. She let the moment sink in, let out a soft sigh, and cocked a hip.

Jean-Claude said, "This isn't what it looks like."

All four of us stared at him.

"Okay," he amended, "it is what it looks like, but let me explain."

"Please," Kevin said. "Go on."

"It's like this," Jean-Claude said, stepping up next to Honey and taking her hand. "We're in love."

His eyes were filled with such earnestness that I could only shake my head.

"How long has this love fest been going on?" Kevin asked, looking between the two.

"A month," Jean-Claude said. "We met when Honey dropped Joey off at the Reaux Construction offices one day. I accidentally backed my car into hers."

Ana scoffed. "Accidentally. Right." Ana not only had first-hand knowledge of Jean-Claude's sneakiness but also the way Reaux men wooed women—she had once dated Jean-Claude's brother.

It had been one of her shortest-lived affairs. The Reaux men weren't known for monogamy. Even though Ana had known so going in, sometimes the Reaux sex appeal could cloud the best of judgments.

Glancing at Honey, I wondered if that was what happened to her, too. She'd been a newlywed of two months when she met him.

"We went for coffee," Honey said, "to sort out insurance information."

"Things escalated from there," Jean-Claude said, shrugging. "You can't fight love."

Ana and I groaned.

Jean-Claude glared. "You can't!"

Kevin zeroed in on Honey. "How did Joey feel about all this love?"

She shifted, cocking her other hip. "Why not ask Delphine about that? I'm sure he told her all about it."

He didn't take her bait. "I want to hear it from you."

Bright pink lips pursed. "As far as I know, he wasn't aware. He was too busy boffing every skirt in town."

"Why stay with him then?" Ana asked.

Kevin glanced at her over his shoulder. "I've got this." He turned back to Honey. "Why stay with him?"

She blinked prettily. "I didn't feel safe leaving."

Tensing, Kevin said, "What does that mean?"

Jean-Claude wrapped his arm around Honey. "Joey said that he'd kill her if she left."

"I didn't really want to die, so I stayed. I figured he'd grow bored of me eventually and leave. I could wait him out."

According to Delphine he'd planned on leaving, but was that true?

I shot a look at Kevin. "Did Joey have a history of violence?"

Honey beat him to the answer. "You name it, he'd been suspected of it." She pressed a hand to the breasts spilling out of her tube top. "Of course, I didn't know that when I married him. He had me fooled."

"He's been a murder suspect?" I asked. This could offer a whole new spin on this case.

Kevin said, "Vehicular homicide. It was an incident that happened about ten years ago in Michigan. His record has been clean for the last couple of years except a DUI six months ago."

"He may have cleaned up his act," Honey narrowed her eyes, "but a tiger can't change its stripes."

Ana said, "Was he involved in illegal dealings? With Reaux Construction?"

Honey twirled a lock of hair around her finger. "He always double deals. Whether he's skimming off the books, scamming on his freelance jobs, or taking shortcuts on the jobsites, he was finding a way to get an extra cut. Bottom line is there's only one person Joey cared about most. Himself."

This made perfect sense to me. He'd obviously tried to con Perry. And if he'd tried it on Perry, then there were probably others out there, too. It was another lead to follow. If Joey had been scamming homeowners, then maybe one of them came after him to get the ultimate revenge.

Then I remembered. *You love her, don't you?*

This case had nothing to do with fraud.

"How'd you meet Joey anyway?" I asked.

Honey looked at Kevin as though asking if she had to answer that. He said, "I'd like to know, too."

"At a bar downtown. I was new to town and he showed me around. Before I knew it, we'd flown off to Vegas to elope." Crocodile tears filled her eyes. "It was the biggest mistake of my life."

"It's okay, baby," Jean-Claude soothed.

The sky overhead had turned the color of a bruise, deep purples and dark blues. The thick air hung heavy with the threat of rain. I glanced at Honey as she was being comforted by Jean-Claude. Something was off about her. She looked the part of a tramp, but there was intelligence in her eyes that couldn't be hidden. She wanted us to believe that she was easily swayed by a slimeball, and that she didn't know his character when she married him...but I'd bet a roll of cookie dough she knew exactly what she was getting into when she married him.

Although why she went through with it was beyond me.

Kevin said, "Where were you both on Wednesday between three forty-five and five p.m.?"

"Together," they said in unison.

Jean-Claude looked at me. "That's why I know Delphine wasn't the last one to see Joey alive. *I* saw him while waiting for Honey to get home from work—we had plans to go out— I saw him pass by the window once or twice. I obviously couldn't come out and tell you that since I didn't want you to know about Honey and me."

Obviously.

I couldn't even believe the hubris needed to pick up your lover in front of the home she shared with her husband.

A raindrop hit Kevin square in the forehead. He flicked it away. "What time was that?"

"About quarter 'til four. I was there early to get Honey, and she got home at four."

Three forty-five. When the call from the pay phone came in.

Kevin's face was unreadable. "Did you see Joey go out around that time?"

"Or anyone else?" I added.

His ponytail swayed as he shook his head. "No."

Kevin switched tactics. "Did Joey tell you if he had any visitors that afternoon, Honey?"

Raindrops had started splashing down all around us giving the concrete a polka-dotted pattern as Honey said, "That's the strange thing. By the time I got home at four, Joey was gone. His phone and wallet were there, but he wasn't. I figured he went off with Delphine, which was fine by me. I didn't have to lie to him about going out with the girls." She crinkled her nose. "I really don't like lying."

Ana made a strangling noise as she held in a laugh. Honey didn't mind cheating but lying was off-limits?

"I didn't see Joey leave," Jean-Claude said, "so he must have gone out the back door."

"Where were you parked?" Kevin asked Jean-Claude.

"In the gas station parking lot across the street. The store probably has footage—you can double-check."

What had happened in those fifteen minutes between Joey receiving that call from a pay phone and Honey returning home? Did Joey leave by his own free will? Or had someone taken him out by force?

Kevin didn't mention that he'd already seen that footage. Instead, he said, "What time did you get home that night, Honey?"

"Midnight. And there was still no sign of Joey. I went to bed. The next day I got up, went to work, came home. Delphine and Plum had called several times and left messages looking for Joey. That's when I realized something was wrong and called the police to report him missing."

"Why not think he just ran off?" Ana asked.

That would have been my first instinct, too.

"Easy. The money in the bank account was still there. He never would have willingly left it—he worked too hard to fleece it."

Drawing in a deep breath, Kevin said, "Can anyone account for you two from four to five?"

"The video footage should show Honey getting into my car at four ten or so. It took fifteen minutes to drive to my place. Then my brother Michel can vouch for us at four thirty," Jean-

Claude said.

Apparently, whoever watched the footage and related its contents to Kevin hadn't mentioned that part about Honey getting into Jean-Claude's car.

"And the pizza delivery guy," Honey added. "At five. We were starving, so we ate early."

"And we went for late-night ice cream, too. The workers there might remember us."

"I am kind of unforgettable," Honey said, fluffing her hair.

"Gag me," Ana mumbled under her breath.

Me, too.

Jean-Claude finally let go of Honey. "We didn't have anything to do with what happened to Joey. Not me, not Honey, not Delphine."

"Who did?" Kevin asked.

I was impressed he didn't say anything about the blood evidence. It was irrefutable. *If* someone hadn't planted it.

Jean-Claude shook his head. "I don't know. I really don't know."

"Do you?" Kevin asked Honey.

One of her fake eyelashes had worked itself loose, and made it look a caterpillar was perched on the corner of her eye. "Anyone. Everyone."

That narrowed it down.

Thunder rumbled in the distance. Dark clouds rolled across the sky, wisps of gray dipping low to the ground.

Right now it was only sprinkling, but I could smell the storm in the air—it was going to be a doozy.

Kevin shot a look upward at the skies. He said, "You two are going to need to come in to the station, answer some more questions."

"We'll be bringing lawyers," Honey said.

She may look like a dumb blonde, but clearly she was not.

"The more the merrier," Kevin responded darkly.

Lightning flashed, and a second later the skies above us opened and poured rain down.

Honey let out a scream, shucked off her shoes, and tried to stuff them into her skin-tight dress. The result was a sight, let me tell you, like something out of the movie *Alien*.

Jean-Claude grabbed her elbow and they jogged away, up the trail.

A bolt of lightning split the sky, and Kevin threw an arm around Ana and me and herded us like sheep back toward the car.

As I turned, I caught sight of a jogger stooped down, tying his shoe, his face turned toward me. And even though he wore sunglasses, I knew he'd been watching me.

I stopped short, and spun around for a double-take.

"What?" Kevin asked.

"Nina, come on!" Ana said, tugging on me as rain drenched us to the skin.

The jogger was gone, his athletic silhouette disappearing

down the trail.

"You seeing ghosts again?" Kevin teased.

I was. Because I could have sworn that jogger was Cain Monahan.

Was it a coincidence that he was here? Watching me?

I didn't think so.

Not at all.

Chapter Fourteen

Kevin had stayed true to his word and followed Ana and me home, though his motives had changed. No longer did he want to make sure we arrived safely—he wanted to speak with Mario.

Rain pummeled the roof of Ana's car as she pulled into Kit's—her—driveway and looked at me. "Smile at him a lot. He won't be so cranky."

Usually I enjoyed the sound of rain against a metal roof, but right now it only added to my anxiety.

I couldn't help but think about Cain Monahan and wonder if he was following me. But the more I thought about it, the more I realized how foolish the notion was. I mean, he'd been dressed in running gear. If he had been following me, he couldn't have known I'd end up at the park. He'd simply been there. Running. And saw me.

That's all.

Except my instinct told me differently.

Then there was Jean-Claude and Honey. The thought occurred to me that they could have concocted an elaborate story about Joey's sudden "disappearance." It was clear that both had motive for wanting him dead.

Could my lover-not-fighter friend have been pushed too far?

My instincts said no to that theory. Jean-Claude wasn't a violent man. The only situation where I could see him losing his cool would be in self-defense. Or protecting someone else—like Honey.

But if that were the case, he'd simply report it and let the police sort out the truth. He certainly wouldn't frame his cousin.

I just couldn't see it.

Besides, the surveillance footage should prove to be his alibi.

My instincts also told me it was someone close to Joey who'd killed him. His murder was too personal. There was anger behind the motive. Whoever killed him wanted him to suffer—and to humiliate him. Stuffing him into a tree...who did that sort of thing?

But if Mario was ruled out and Honey and Jean-Claude were ruled out...who was left?

Delphine and her crew. Plum, Bear, Ethan.

One of them was guilty. I was sure of it.

At this point I leaned toward Bear. He had a thing for Delphine. Jealousy could have precipitated this murder. Framing Delphine might have been Bear's way of making her pay for rejecting him.

"Do you think I have good instincts?" I asked Ana.

"No."

"Thanks for sugarcoating it."

"No problem."

I pushed open the door. Kevin had pulled into my driveway behind my work truck.

I told Ana I'd see her later and made a mad dash across the street. I didn't know why I bothered to sprint—I was already soaked to the bone. As I ran, I noticed that the yellow crime scene tape was missing from Mario and Perry's house.

That was good news—the scene had been cleared, and I could get to work in the back yard as soon as this weather broke.

Lightning flashed and I kicked up my pace. I didn't slow down as I passed Kevin's SUV and headed straight for the porch.

I heard his footsteps splashing behind me as thunder cracked. As I reached for the door, there was humor in his voice as he said, "You run like a girl."

"I am a girl."

"I noticed. Especially in that wet T-shirt."

I looked down. Not again! "For Pete's sake!"

Tossing an arm over my chest, I said, "You could have the decency to look away."

He waggled his eyebrows. "I could."

"Ugh."

I shoved open the door to find Maria and Perry cozied up on the couch. They barely flicked a glance in our direction—their attention was firmly focused on the TV. There was some sort of show on featuring young pageant girls.

Save me now.

"What're you two watching?" I asked.

"*Small-Town Crown*," Perry said. "It's genius."

"Genius," Maria echoed. "Small-town girls compete at local pageants for a sash, cash, and crown. The winners of each of those pageants then go on to a national pageant for even bigger prizes. And they aren't allowed to wear a speck of makeup or fake teeth or any of the usual pageant stuff. Aren't they so cute?"

I glanced at the screen. The little girl strutting down the runway had her hair teased out like Tina Turner in the "What's love got to do with it?" video. She grinned, her jack-o'-lantern smile endearing. I had to admit she was adorable.

Maria rubbed her belly. "I could see my little girl doing pageants. Maybe not this one, though. A little mascara does wonders for eyes."

Perry's eyes lit up. "She'd win, too. If she has your cheek bones—those other girls wouldn't stand a chance."

Those other girls. The imaginary ones. "No," I said to her. "No pageants."

Maria scoffed. "You're not the boss of me, Nina Quinn."

"We'll let Mom settle this."

Maria huffed but didn't say anything.

"Where have you been?" Perry asked, finally noticing that I wasn't alone. "Has there been a new development?"

Kevin kept glancing at my chest as though wishing I'd drop my arms. "You could say that."

"I need to talk to Mario," Kevin said.

Perry snapped his gaze to me. "Did you rat him out?"

"Noooo. The video footage from the UDF across the street from Joey Miller's townhouse did that."

"I just have a couple of questions for him," Kevin said.

Maria tried to straighten but finally gave up and leaned back into the couch cushions. "Is he a suspect?"

"Is he here?" Kevin asked, ignoring her.

Perry let out a dramatic sigh. "No, he's not. He decided he'd be happier staying at Kit's house. He's over there."

"Alone?" I asked.

"He has Kit," Perry said.

"And Ana," Maria added. "And BeBe."

"But not you?" I asked him.

"I don't want to talk about it," he said.

Maria was more than happy to spill the beans. "They had a big fight. About that tie."

"He's being silly," Perry said. "I'd be proud if he had a secret admirer."

"Sure you would," I said.

"What? I would. It's an honor."

"Remember when the waiter flirted with Mario at his birthday dinner and you tripped the poor man when he walked past you?"

He waved away the memory. "Mario's made his choice. He can stay with Kit for all I care."

It was going to be a long night. I left the three of them in the living room and scurried off to the laundry room to get a towel from the dryer. I wrapped it around me and came back into the living room to find Gracie growling at Kevin.

He growled back.

A puddle appeared on the floor.

"Let me walk you out," I said to Kevin.

"Am I leaving?"

"Yes."

"Since you're going out, can you take Gracie for a walk?" Maria asked.

Perry said, "If you see Mario and he asks for me, tell him I don't miss him at all."

"Save yourself," I whispered to Kevin.

He spun and headed for the door.

I scooped up Gracie, stepped over the puddle, and followed Kevin outside. The rain had ebbed a bit but still fell steadily. "I've been thinking about who might have killed Joey and really think it's someone from Delphine's crew. They all had problems with him, and Bear..."

"Delphine has already been charged, Nina. The evidence

hasn't changed."

I set Gracie on the porch. She walked back to the front door and whimpered. "You're not releasing her?"

"She went back, but used the back door this time. Maybe they left together that way and she killed him at her house..."

"You don't know that."

"You don't know she didn't."

"Aren't you even going to look at the rest of the crew? Have you looked into their alibis at all? Questioned them?"

His tone was hard, unyielding. "Stay out of it, Nina."

I was getting sick of him saying that to me.

He added, "You're going to have to trust me."

Ah. Well. That was going to be a problem. He hadn't quite gained back all my trust yet after the whole cheating thing. I bit my lip and adjusted my towel. "I don't think it can hurt to investigate them a little bit."

"I'll talk to you later," he said, stepping into the rain.

"Hey," I said.

He turned.

"Mario and Perry's house... It's cleared?"

Rain slid down his face. "It's clear. You're free to get to work. The sooner the better."

"Why's that?"

"Because it'll keep you too busy to investigate my suspects."

Damn! He knew me too well. But... I pointed at him. "Ha!

Your suspects? So you are looking into their alibis?"

"Bye, Nina."

"You'll tell me what you find, right?" I called after him as he crossed the street, on his way to Kit's to talk with Mario.

He shot a hand into the air and waved me off.

I smiled. I'd get those alibis, all right.

One way or another.

Chapter Fifteen

Early the next morning, Maria found me sitting on the front porch swing. I held the seat steady and at an angle so it would be easier for her to sit. The chains connected to the porch ceiling creaked as she settled in, and she smiled as we swayed.

For a second in the morning light, she looked like her old self. At peace. Then she pierced me with a blue stare and said, "I need that envelope, Nina. I don't know where you have it hidden—I'm pretty sure it's not here. Is it at your office? I need it back."

I knew she'd spent a good portion of the day before looking for the ultrasound results. She hadn't made a mess during her search, but everything was a little bit off. The corner of a picture tilted, the edge of the bed out of alignment, the towels in the linen closet askew.

"You can't have it back." I grabbed my mug of coffee from the side table as we swung past it.

"Do you know that there are baby pageants? How am I supposed to plan ahead if I don't know the gender of my baby?"

"Maria, you'll know soon enough."

She pouted. "It's *my* baby."

"You made me promise. Pinkie swear and everything."

"You promised Perry you wouldn't rat out Mario and look what happened."

"I didn't say anything. Kevin saw the footage."

"Sure, sure."

"Don't make me leave you out here. You know you can't get out of this swing by yourself."

"You wouldn't dare."

"Try me."

She harrumphed, folded her arms above her rounded stomach, and looked off in the distance.

The silent treatment.

It might work on others, but the quiet was music to my ears.

Across the street, at Mario and Perry's place, I saw Riley step out the front door carrying a pipe. He was there helping Kit try to get the plumbing situation worked out. They'd started early—just after dawn—and Kit was motivated to finish the job today.

Apparently one night with Mario under his roof was quite enough.

I'd had a fitful night's sleep. Between Maria trying to find a comfortable position, my thoughts about the murder and Cain Monahan...I'd barely slept at all.

"You know what I was thinking about this morning?" Maria said.

She wasn't one to suffer in silence for long.

"Shiny tiaras?"

"Besides that. I was thinking about Seth Thiessen. Do you know why?"

"Because the coroner's investigator looks just like him?"

"No, because you said his name in your sleep last night."

I took a sip of coffee. "Did I? Strange."

Her eyes softened. "Maybe you should call Peter and talk this out. Obviously this coroner guy has stirred up some old feelings of yours. You were young when he died—maybe you didn't know how to grieve back then."

"I grieved." I remembered the tears well. "It's just that he looks so much like him."

Softly, she said, "He's gone, Nina."

I didn't tell her about seeing him at the park yesterday. She'd surely chalk it up to me being delusional or obsessive or something. But I knew it had been him.

County offices were closed on Sundays, so I planned to drop in on Cain tomorrow.

"Do you remember anything about the plane crash?" I asked. "Did authorities ever figure out what happened?"

"You're not going to let this go, are you?"

"Not 'til I see his eyes."

Sighing, she said, "I was littler than you when the crash

151

happened, only seven or eight. I don't remember much at all. But..."

"But what?"

"Do you remember Kiera Marsh? She was on my junior cheer squad."

Maria had been a cheering dynamo and a member of a private team even in elementary school.

I shook my head. The name wasn't the least bit familiar.

"Well, once shortly after the crash I heard her talking about how her father said that the plane crash was a shame but not a shock, considering the reputation of the The Black Fox. It always stuck with me, that comment. Mostly because her dad was a Cincinnati cop and she was always going on and on about how important he was."

"The Black Fox? Seth's dad's pub?"

She shrugged. "I didn't understand it, either. And when I told Mom about it she just told me to shush. You can ask her about it. I'm sure she remembers more about that time than any of us."

"I could if she weren't out at sea with no phone." My mother didn't do email, either—she was a technophobe. My father, however, loved gadgets. I could send him a message. The sooner the better. I slowed the swing and hopped off. Holding out a hand to Maria, I helped her off. "How was your blood pressure this morning?"

"The same," she said, flexing her swollen fingers.

I was surprised she hadn't badgered her doctor into moving

up the date of her induction. But then again, I knew how nervous she was about becoming a mom, so she was probably clinging to these last few days of relative freedom.

I wasn't worried. Maria was going to be a great mom. Underneath all her hairspray and egoism, she had a big heart that had plenty of room for a baby. "You want some breakfast?"

She waddled ahead of me. "I thought you'd never ask. I'm starving. I was beginning to question your hostess skills."

I let out a sigh. "When's Nate coming?"

"Tomorrow," she said and threw a smile over her shoulder. "Aren't you so glad you get me for another night?"

"Thrilled," I said, following her inside. "Just thrilled."

***

Kit wiped beads of sweat off his bald tattooed head and said, "Why'd they buy this dump?"

I glanced around the dark basement, lit with what seemed like a forty-watt bulb. The cement floor had been jack-hammered open, revealing roots wrapped around broken pipes.

Riley said, "It was cheap."

"Dirt cheap," I added.

Disgusted, he frowned at the scene before him. "It should have been free. I don't know how it passed inspection."

"Easy. It was sold as is."

He let out a curse.

I gestured to a broken pipe. "Is this beyond your area of expertise? Should we call in a plumber?"

"Nothing is beyond my area of expertise, Nina."

"Yeah," Riley echoed.

"Fine, fine," I said, looking between the two of them. "If you need me, I'll be outside."

The ground was too wet to get much done, but I could start marking out the design plan and make sure all the supplies had been delivered for tomorrow's big makeover. If I was especially motivated, I could start pulling up the current plantings. Fortunately, there weren't many of those.

I trudged up the basement stairs and found Mario pacing the kitchen. Dark circles shadowed the skin beneath his brown eyes, and he looked like he'd had as much sleep as I did.

"I don't care how Perry's doing," he snapped.

I put up my hands in surrender. "Then you won't care that he barely got a wink of sleep and has already eaten a dozen cookies, two cannoli, and three doughnuts all before noon."

He scoffed. "He's probably been drinking coffee by the gallon, too. He knows he shouldn't, because it gives him the shakes, but without me there he has no self-control."

"You probably don't care, too, that he misses you."

There was a beat of silence before he said, "Nope, I don't."

I wasn't buying it for a second. Mario cared—a lot—just as

Perry did. They simply needed to sit down and hash out their grievances. Maybe Maria could mediate. She was pretty good at it, I had to admit.

A flash of white caught my eye as a van pulled into the driveway and another car behind it. I peeked out the window and gasped as Plum hopped out of the van and Bear and Ethan out of the car. They started gathering tools. "What are they doing here?"

Color rose up Mario's cheeks. "Plum called my cell last night, asking to finish the job. Cut her previous price in half."

"Oh, Mario."

"What?" he said defensively. "The sooner this work gets done, the better. They're motivated to do it right, are willing to work on weekends, and promise it will be done by next Monday. I've taken this whole upcoming week off to supervise. Nothing else will go wrong."

I reached over and knocked on the wooden cabinet.

"What are you doing?" he asked.

"Knocking on wood. Saying nothing else is going to go wrong is just asking for something else to go wrong."

He stared at me.

"It is!"

He kept staring. Finally, he said, "Are you working out back today?"

I said, "You've been hanging around with Maria too much. You're picking up her bad manners."

"She's a lovely woman."

I groaned and walked out the back door, stopping short when I nearly bumped into Bear Broward and Ethan Onderko. They'd been here approximately two minutes and were already taking a smoke break on the back deck. I scooted around them and picked up my can of bright orange marking spray.

Ethan flicked his lighter on and off as he watched me.

Bear just stared.

I figured this was a great time to ask them some questions, but I couldn't quite find any words.

Bear broke the silence. "You really gonna have this yard changed by tomorrow night?"

"Completely changed," I said.

Several pallets of paver bricks had been dropped in the side yard. Decking material was sitting out front, and the local nursery I used was due to drop off all the plants, flowers, shrubs, and trees tomorrow morning. My crew would be hard at work bright and early.

"I don't believe it," Bear said.

"Me, either," Ethan added, still flicking that lighter.

"You'll see," I said, as I marked out a planting bed near the existing deck and wished with all my might that they'd go away.

I cleared my throat. "I'm a little surprised to see you guys back...so soon." I added the soon part so they wouldn't catch on that I wished they'd go away forever.

"Gotta make ends meet," Bear said.

Ethan nodded. *Flick, flick, flick.*

I tried to think of something else to ask them and found I had plenty of questions. Where'd you grow up, how well did you know Joey, have you ever killed anyone...but I didn't really want to converse with them. My sleuthing skills had crawled into a hole and refused to come out. These two scared the bejeebers out of me.

Kevin would be laughing his ass off if he could see me now.

The back slider opened and Plum popped her head out. "Break's over. We've got work to do."

Ethan stubbed out his cigarette on the deck stair and tossed it into the grass. He kept staring at me as he skulked into the house.

Bear flicked his cigarette too, and heaved himself off the step. His footsteps thudded on the deck as he crossed it.

I let out a deep sigh of relief until a voice from behind startled me.

"Miz Quinn?"

I jumped back, spun around, and aimed the spray at the person who'd snuck up behind me.

Mr. Cabrera wore a bright yellow button down covered in strawberries and a sheepish grin. "Didn't mean to scare you."

I didn't even try to deny that he had. "I didn't hear you come up. Are you feeling better, Mr. Cabrera?"

"Yes and no. That's why I wanted to talk to you. Do you have a second?"

I glanced around at the yard. It could wait. But as my gaze

fell on the discarded cigarette butts, I had an idea. "Give me a sec."

I ran into Mario's kitchen, rifled through drawers until I found two plastic baggies. Back outside, I used a stick to flip the butts into the bags.

Mr. Cabrera watched me with one bushy eyebrow raised.

"Shhh," I said to him.

"Didn't say a word."

I tucked the baggies into the pocket of my cargo pants and sat down on the back step. He settled in next to me, and I waited for him to speak his mind.

He wrung his hands, glanced at me out of the corner of his eye, and said, "I need your help, Nina."

Chapter Sixteen

Operation Help Mr. Cabrera was on hold until later in the afternoon—we'd made plans to meet up at three. What he wanted from me was fairly simple, but I couldn't help but wonder if his actions would be too little too late.

The sun shone high overhead as Coby Fowler, one of my employees, dropped off the company bobcat. He stuck around to chainsaw and chip what was left of the tree that had held Joey Miller's body.

The sound of the wood chipper was grating on my nerves, so I snuck inside to steal a peek at Kit's progress in the basement.

I found Plum patching woodwork at the top of the steps and eased around her.

I crept down the steps, just enough to see Kit and Riley kneeling on the dug-up floor elbow deep in what I hoped was muddy water. Bear and Ethan were in the corner, installing a new water heater. Mario stood off to the side, keeping a close eye on everything but not getting close enough to get dirty.

I heard Bear say to him, "So what did you do then?"

"I moved out!"

"And in with me," Kit grumbled.

Bear paused in what he was doing. "Why'd you do that?"

"I couldn't take another moment of how gleeful he was that he had a secret admirer. It's bad enough that he received the gifts, but he actually put the tie on last night."

"Dude," Bear said, shaking his enormous head. "That ain't right."

"I know," Mario agreed. "That's why I left."

Kit tossed an irritated look at Mario, who didn't appear to notice.

"But you still, you know, dig him, right?" Bear asked.

Ethan handed Bear a wrench, and seemed more focused on the job than the conversation.

Mario grumped. "I suppose."

"Then you should go talk to him. Make up. Life's too short, man."

I smiled at what I was hearing, this little pep talk.

"Maybe," Mario said.

"I think it's a good idea," Kit added.

Riley nodded.

Ethan continued to ignore everyone.

I decided now wasn't the best time to barge in, so I backtracked up the stairs.

Plum said, "They having any luck down there?"

Today she wore a skin-tight Reaux Construction v-necked

tee and jeans. The vee of the tee had been altered to be even deeper than normal to accommodate her boobage. Her hair had been scraped back into a tight ponytail, and she wore enough makeup to keep Sephora in business for a long time to come.

"Define luck," I said.

"That good, eh?"

"Looks like Bear and Ethan have the water heater under control."

"That's good."

"But don't ask about the pipe."

"I'll call my plumbing contractor." Her dark brown eyes narrowed on me and she leaned in a little.

"Bear's giving Mario love advice," I said, fishing for more information on him. "Good advice, too."

"He's a good guy."

Was he? Or had he lured Joey out of his house and killed him with a bedazzled hammer?

She patched a hole, then looked at me. "Jean-Claude mentioned you were something of a matchmaker. True?"

"Me? No."

"You didn't set up your neighbor with that one lady and also the girl at your office with that one guy...?"

She was talking about Mr. Cabrera and Brickhouse and Tam and Ian. "Well, not intentionally. Not really. And my neighbor's relationship isn't going so well."

"What about the girl at the office?"

"Happily cohabitating." Tam had been together with DEA agent Ian for almost a year now. Together they were raising Tam's daughter, Nic.

"Can I ask you something, then. Girl to girl?"

I fidgeted. "Um, sure."

"How do you get a guy to notice you? Right now I'm invisible."

"To Bear, you mean?"

Her eyes widened in shock. "How'd you know?"

"Lucky guess," I said, not wanting to get into the fact that she'd practically ripped her heart out of her chest the day before and laid it on the table for him.

"He seems to only want Delphine." She rolled her eyes.

"Probably because she doesn't want him," I said.

Plump lips pursed. "You think?"

"It's possible. Some guys like the chase. But you'd probably be best just to talk to him. Some guys are also dense and can't see what's in front of them."

She nodded. "I get it. I suppose it can't hurt any worse to try."

Suddenly I felt sorry for her, this tough girl. It was never easy to open your heart up to a guy who may or may not want it. "Probably not."

"Thanks."

"If Kit comes up, can you tell him I had to run an errand

and that I'll check in later?"

"No problem, but we'll be leaving soon, too. We'll be back early tomorrow, though. Oh, one more thing."

Geez.

"Earlier I heard Mario talking about a fight he had with Joey. On the day Joey died? He was telling the guys about it..."

Kevin must have completely cleared him for him to be speaking freely about it.

"Anyway, he said he heard someone else in the house. A guy. And that he recognized the voice but couldn't place it." Thick lashes framed her eyes as they narrowed. "Your husband, the police guy, does he know who that is yet?"

Ah. I wondered if she had the same suspicions about Bear as I did. "He's my ex and doesn't tell me stuff like that. Sorry."

Absently, she nodded. "Okay."

I hurried out the front door before she could ask me anything else, like for any more relationship advice. Because considering the state of my love life, I was probably the least qualified to give it.

An understatement to be sure.

I spotted Mr. Cabrera chatting with Perry on my front porch. As I neared, Mr. C. said, "Perry's agreed to come along, too. You ready to go?"

"As I'll ever be," I said.

It was time to get Operation Help Mr. Cabrera underway.

***

Turned out we weren't quite as ready to go as we'd thought. First, Maria came out and asked me to walk Gracie, then when I was done with that, she made me wait while she wrote out a grocery list so I could stop at the store on the way home. By the time we backed out of the driveway, she was tucked in for a nap, and the Reaux Construction crew was packing up for the day.

Kit was still working—he was determined to get Mario back into his own house as soon as humanly possible.

I couldn't blame him. Mario was a bit high-strung, especially when he was fighting with Perry.

Fortunately, our destination was only a few blocks away, and as the bell tinkled on the door of The Gem Shop, Mr. Cabrera froze in the doorway.

Perry gave him a good push, sending him tumbling inside.

"Donatelli!" the man behind the counter gushed. "Long time, no see."

"Hey Saul."

"Nina," he grabbed his heart, "my bella! It's been too long." He grabbed my hand to kiss my knuckles.

"Hi, Saul." I wrenched my hand free. Saul Simeon was as smarmy as men came, but he meant no harm. I'd known him just shy of forever—he was an old family friend. His gray hair had been slicked back, and he wore a badly tailored suit and gaudy gold rings on both hands.

Saul rubbed his hands together, the rings clinking. "To what do I owe this pleasure? How can I help you folks today?"

Perry had already wandered off, his attention diverted by something shiny. I poked Mr. Cabrera in the ribcage.

He coughed and said, "I'm here to look at rings. Eng—" He coughed some more. "Engagement rings."

"You sly old dog!" Saul cried. "You're finally going to tie the knot again. Who's the lucky ball and chain? Is it Ursula?"

Weakly, Mr. Cabrera nodded.

"Lucky lady!"

Mr. Cabrera looked a little pale as Saul motioned him over to a display case. Behind the glass, dozens of diamond rings winked under the bright lights.

I linked my arm in Mr. Cabrera's and leaned in to whisper, "You love her, right?"

Wiping his brow, he said, "More than anything."

"Then you're doing the right thing."

He frowned at me. "Easy for you to say. You're not tying yourself down for the rest of your life."

"Suck it up, Mr. Cabrera. If you want your happily ever after, this is the way to do it."

"What kind of moral support are you?" he asked, a horrified expression in his eyes.

"One that's going to tell you the truth."

"Oh. My. God. Nina, look at these cufflinks," Perry gushed. "They're to die for. To. Die. For!"

I said, "We're supposed to be helping Mr. Cabrera, remember?"

"Yeah, yeah," he said, his eyes glued to the display case.

Saul was pulling out little velvet boxes and setting them on the counter. "Do you know what style Ursula likes?"

Mr. Cabrera said, "An affordable one."

I elbowed him again.

"Ow!" He stepped aside. "Why'd you do that?"

"This is no time to be cheap."

"No," Saul quickly agreed. "It isn't."

"Pony up, Mr. Cabrera," Perry said.

Mr. C. groaned.

I leaned down and examined the rings. "It needs to be something simple. Ursula is not a frou-frou woman. But she has style...she won't want something cheap." I threw Mr. Cabrera a look.

He looked like he wanted to toss his cookies again.

Saul held up a finger. "I have just the selection." He reached into the case and pulled out a tray of rings elegantly pinned to velvet.

All were round diamonds in different settings. Some stood on their own, and some were encircled with smaller diamonds. Some had diamond bands, some had designed bands, some had plain.

"Do you see one you like?" I asked.

One of Mr. Cabrera's eyebrows lifted. "Meh. Not quite. He

tapped the glass. That one."

Saul's eyes lit up and he greedily reached into the case. I smiled as he brought out the ring Mr. Cabrera had pointed to. It was perfect. Absolutely perfect.

Saul held it up. "A one carat oval cut center diamond, surrounded by a half carat of smaller round diamonds that also trail down the platinum band. It is—" he kissed his fingers "—sublime."

Perry wandered over and *ooohed.* "I've never seen an oval diamond before."

"It's unique," Mr. Cabrera announced proudly, "just like my Ursula."

I nudged him. "That's the spirit."

"Wrap it up," Mr. Cabrera said in one quick breath.

"Don't you want to know how much?" Saul asked.

Mr. C. pulled out his wallet and passed over a credit card. "No. I don't want to change my mind."

I intercepted the card as he handed it over. "But, I'm sure you'll give Mr. Cabrera the friends and family discount, right, Saul?"

His beady eyes gleamed. "Of course! Of course!" He snatched the card.

Perry cleared his throat. "How much for the mother of pearl and ruby cufflinks?"

"Ah!" Saul practically salivated. He pulled out the cufflinks in question and placed them on the counter. "You have exquisite taste."

"I know," Perry said.

"These are also unique, a trait reflected in the price."

I sighed. "Saul..."

He shot me an irritated glance. "Twelve hundred."

"I don't think they're in your budget," I said to Perry.

He looked between me and the cufflinks. "I hate the budget."

"Think of your house. The quartz countertop. The hand-scraped oak floors."

He pouted—he'd definitely been taking lessons from Maria. "Mario would kill me."

"Yes," I said. "Yes, he would. And you're not exactly on his favorite-person list right now."

"You want?" Saul said to him.

Perry let out a deep sigh. "Yes, but I can't have them. Not today."

Saul *tsk*ed. "Such a shame. I'm unsure they'll be here when you return."

Perry shot me a look.

"Saul," I said.

He said, "You can't blame a man for trying." Picking up the ring, he swept through swinging doors with Mr. Cabrera's credit card firmly in hand.

"I don't feel so well," Mr. C. said.

"Me, either," Perry added, peering at his beloved cufflinks.

I bit my tongue from lashing out at either of them.

Saul was back in a jiff, had Mr. Cabrera sign the credit card receipt, and handed over a small bag.

Perry moped his way to the car. "When are you going to ask Ursula the big question?"

"I don't know," he said.

I turned on the car. "I wouldn't wait too long."

He clasped the bag to his chest. "I need to come up with a plan. Do something special. I've waited this long, so I don't suppose another day will matter."

As I headed home, I hoped that he wasn't wrong about that.

Chapter Seventeen

Later that night I stood at the kitchen counter chopping green chilies for the enchiladas I was making for dinner. Maria and Perry were back to watching episodes of *Small-Town Crown* (they were going to need a twelve-step program soon), and I had Riley working on setting the table. After dinner he'd head back to Kevin's condo across town—it was a school night and the weekend visit was drawing to a close.

My heart clenched a little at the fact that he was leaving again, and I wondered if it was ever going to get easier. Probably not. Then next thing I knew he'd be headed off to college. Then married. Then babies.

Heaven help me, but the thought of Kevin being a grandpa did make me smile.

As I slid the chilies into a mixing bowl, I kept throwing looks at Riley.

"What?" he asked. "Why do you keep looking at me like that?"

After snatching a dishtowel that hung from the oven door handle, I dried my hands. "There will be plenty of extra for dinner if you want to invite anyone over."

His eyes flashed. "You want me to call Dad?"

I whipped the dishtowel in his direction. "I meant Layla. How long have you two been dating?"

"We're not dating." He set forks next to the plates. "We're *seeing* each other."

"*Ohhhh*," I said sarcastically. "Now I understand. How long have you been *seeing* each other? Has your dad met her?"

"A little while and no."

Riley lacked the ability to be forthcoming on just about any topic, but this was pushing his secrecy to a new level. "I can't help but feel as though you're keeping her from us. Like you're embarrassed of your family or something."

From the living room Maria shouted, "Oh my God, is she wearing a purple sequin jumper? No one wears purple sequins."

"Hookers do," Perry said. "I saw one last week, ho'ing downtown."

Maria said, "That's disturbing."

He said, "The sequins or the ho?"

"Both," she answered. "Both."

Riley set a stack of napkins on the table, looked at me straight on and said, "Your point?"

Okay, our family was a tiddly bit embarrassing. Most were, though, so that was no excuse. "I'd like to meet her."

"Maybe," he said evasively.

Cheddar cheese went into the bowl along with some shredded chicken and garlic. "*Maybe* next weekend or *maybe* if hell freezes over?"

"We'll see," he said loftily and walked out of the kitchen.

I filled a dozen tortillas, set them in a baking pan, covered them with cheese and then foil and stuck the pan in the oven. I hopped onto a stool and slid my laptop over to see if my father had written back to me. I logged onto my email, but there were no new messages.

I drummed my fingers on the counter and finally called up a search engine. I typed in The Black Fox + Eric Thiessen.

I had to pay to read several articles that had been archived in the *Cincinnati Enquirer*. As I let what I read settle in my brain, I thought back to my childhood. I'd never associated anything bad with the Thiessen family, but these articles revealed that Mr. Thiessen's business had ties to a white supremacist gang. The week before the plane crash, he'd testified in a federal court about a murder he'd witnessed behind his pub.

The next week, he and his family were dead.

A shiver went up my spine. It was against one of my personal commandments to believe in coincidences.

However, if the plane had been tampered with, I didn't understand why there weren't more articles about the accident. Why hadn't anyone been charged with killing the family?

I was stewing over it when Perry walked into the kitchen and sat next to me. He propped his elbow on the counter and settled his chin into his hand. Sadness was etched into every line on his face—at least the ones he hadn't Botoxed.

I patted his back. "It'll all be okay."

"I screwed up, Nina."

Closing the laptop screen, I glanced over at him and was dismayed to see the depth of regret in his eyes. I couldn't very well agree with him without further hurting his feelings, so I waited for him to explain.

"I saw Kit and Mario leave the house earlier," he said.

Much to Kit's dismay, the pipes still weren't fixed, so it was another night of Mario under his roof.

"So I snuck over to check out the progress. I couldn't get in. Mario had changed the locks."

"No!"

"Yes! I mean, the back slider never locks right, so I was still able to get inside, but still. He changed the locks!"

"Can he do that? It's your house, too."

Drawing an imaginary circle on the counter, he said, "Actually it's not. Mario paid for it. I can barely save enough money to make my car payment."

He was one of the biggest spenders I knew. "Oh, Perry."

"The worst part is that this is all my fault. I had to gloat over those presents I got."

True. He had gloated. But I tried to make him feel better. "They were nice gifts."

"I know," he said, sliding me a surreptitious glance. "I picked them out."

It took a second for his words to register. "Wait. You what?"

"I picked them out. I sent the presents to myself, Nina."

"Perry Owens!"

He winced. "I wanted to make Mario realize what a catch I am."

"You've been hanging out with Mr. Cabrera too much."

Nodding, he said, "But what do I do now? I've screwed everything up."

I crossed the kitchen and grabbed two wine glasses and filled them to the rim. I slid one over to him. "You have to talk to him. Confess." I recalled what Bear had said to Mario. "I think he'll be receptive. You two love each other. You'll figure this out."

"You think?"

"Yes. But it wouldn't hurt for you to compromise a little in the relationship, like Maria advised. Life's not about material possessions."

"I suppose I can compromise. A little. I'll talk to him."

"Well, don't wait too long," I advised for the second time that afternoon.

He guzzled the wine. "I'll talk to him first thing in the morning, before I go to work. And I'll return all the presents, too."

"Perry!" Maria called. "She dropped the baton! She dropped the damn baton!"

Maria really needed to calm down or she was going to put herself into labor.

Scooting off his stool, he grabbed his glass and held it up to me in a half-hearted salute. "You're the best, Nina Quinn."

"Yeah, yeah."

"No, you are."

I fluffed my hair. "How about you show me?"

His eyebrows shot up. "What do you have in mind?"

"Sell me the vintage watch instead of taking it back to the store? Father's Day is coming up, and my dad would love it."

He gulped.

"At a discount."

"How much of a discount?"

"Steep."

Taking a deep breath, he said, "Fine, but I'm not happy about it."

I said, "But I'm the best, remember?"

"The best bamboozler." He kissed my cheek.

As I watched him stride out of the kitchen, I could only hope that once Perry explained everything that Mario would give him a second chance.

That seemed to be a theme around here lately, second chances.

Mr. Cabrera and Brickhouse.

Perry and Mario.

Kevin and me?

I wasn't ready to make that decision but knew I'd have to soon.

Really soon.

***

There was something so soothing to me about early mornings at my office, even when that morning fell on a Monday.

The building was quiet—no one else was in yet—as I sat behind my desk and sipped my coffee. My gaze kept falling on the envelope sitting inside a plastic bag that lay askew on my blotter.

The plastic bag was a necessity because it had been hiding inside the planter of Tam's African violet, Sassy. Inside the thin folds of the paper envelope were Maria's ultrasound results.

I wouldn't have pulled the envelope from Sassy's pot except for the fact that I discovered my office key in the wrong spot on my key ring when I got to work today. It was usually nestled between my truck key and the storage shed key...but not today.

Which made me think that someone had "borrowed" the key at some point over the weekend. Probably to have a copy made so the culprit could break in and search for these ultrasound results while I was busy all day at Mario and Perry's house.

This left me little choice.

Setting my mug on the desk, I snapped open the plastic baggie and took out the envelope. I tapped it twice on its edge and tore a thin line across the short end and shook the piece of paper out onto my desk. It had been folded in quarters so the writing wouldn't be visible if held up to a light, and as I picked it up, my fingers ached to unfurl the note.

But I knew I couldn't. There's no way I could keep the baby's gender a secret. Before I could change my mind, I spun in my swivel chair and fed the note into the crosscut shredder. After the blades stopped churning, I scooped up the confetti and dropped it into a pile on my desk. I then took my scissors and began chopping the confetti into even smaller pieces.

I looked up as the front door chimed and Tam called out, "You have to tell me what happened with Ursula! Why did she call me this morning and tell me she's going away for a month?"

"A month?" I asked as Tam appeared in my doorway. "She told me two weeks."

"She bamboozled you."

Hmm. A lot of that going on lately.

Tam Oliver was the spitting image of a young Queen Elizabeth and had the haughty mannerisms to match. Perry even styled her hair in an old-fashioned style that complimented Tam's (and the Queen's) bone structure perfectly. However, when Tam spoke there was no mistaking the Midwest twang in her voice. And I seriously doubted that the Queen had the computer-hacking skills Tam possessed.

I sliced through some more confetti. "She and Mr. Cabrera had a falling out."

"Another one?"

"It's bad this time, but I have hope he can fix it." I told her all about the big fight, and how Mr. Cabrera had bought an engagement ring.

Tam's eyes grew wide. "He's going to propose? When? Because she's packing to leave for a cruise that sets off tomorrow morning. She's flying down to Florida tonight. I think she said it was an eight o'clock flight."

"I'm sure he'll be nosing around the work site today, so I'll let him know that he's running out of time."

Tam smiled and rubbed her hands. "Ursula will be thrilled."

I hoped so. I really did.

Tam said, "What're you doing? Arts and crafts?"

"Of a sort." I explained. "If Maria finds the results, it'll be a lesson in patience to get all the pieces put back together again."

Tam frowned. "You should have just told her. It's her baby."

"Not you, too! She made me promise."

"Nina, if there's one thing you should know it's that promises are made to be broken."

Tam had a rough life growing up, and Nic's dad was better off out of her life. But I thought things had been going well with her and Ian. "You okay? You and Ian?"

She smiled. "Right as rain. Knock on wood." She tapped on

the door jamb. "It's just that sometimes doing what's right means not being so righteous all the time."

I stuck my tongue out at her.

She laughed.

"Speaking of Ian," I said.

Rolling her eyes, she said, "What now? Does this have to do with Joey Miller's murder?"

She knew me too well. I swiveled in my seat again and fished through my tote. I came up with three plastic baggies and held them up. "I have some extra work for you if you're willing?"

"Standard terms?" she asked, stepping closer to get a better look at my bevy of evidence.

"Yes. One hour babysitting for every hour you work on the side project."

She held up one of the bags—the one that held Bear's cigarette butt. "Two hours. I'm going to have to get Ian involved, and you know how he hates that."

"And I know you love to persuade him."

She blushed. "You're right about that, but still."

"Okay, an hour and a half."

"Deal."

"The cigarettes are from Bear and Ethan from Delphine's crew. I don't need their DNA run or anything that technical—just their fingerprints."

"And this?" She held up Cain Monahan's business card. "A

coroner's investigator? You don't really think he's involved..."

"That one's personal."

Her eyebrows shot up. "Oh?"

"Not like that," I said. "It's just... A long story."

"I have time."

"Well, I don't. I have to get over to Mario and Perry's. One more favor?"

"Two hours."

"Talk about bamboozling."

She smiled. "Where do you think Ursula learned it? What is it you need?"

"I tried to do a search on Joey Miller, but his name was too common. Is there any way you—"

Holding up a hand, she cut me off and went searching in her tote bag. She finally pulled out a folder and dropped it on my desk. "I had a feeling that you would be asking."

"It's scary how well you know me," I said.

"Terrifying. I'll prorate your hours appropriately." She wiggled her eyebrows and walked out.

As she greeted Sassy, I stared at the manila file. Taking a deep breath, I opened it.

Tam had done well—she even included a current picture, all his mug shots, and his Facebook profile picture. Part of me felt guilty that I used her talents this way, but the other part was just too damn grateful to have the information. Plus, most of what she gleaned was done through public records—she simply had more knowledge about how to weave through the Internet highway than I did.

At least that's what I told myself as guilt continued to prick my conscience.

I checked through the pages of Joey's rap sheet. It seemed he'd covered the whole gamut of crime from petty theft to multiple assaults to vehicular homicide.

I scanned the information Tam had found on the assaults. Most seemed to stem from confrontations with enraged homeowners who realized they'd been conned or from bar-fight incidents. He was no stranger to jails.

Flipping the page, I focused in on the homicide charge—of which he'd been ultimately acquitted. Seemed like Joey's temper had gotten the best of him—not with an irate homeowner or in a love triangle gone wrong (either of which I could easily believe)—but during a road rage incident in Michigan. Long story short was that he'd been tailgating a car on the highway, but when he tried to pass the other car would speed up, too. Both cars sped along until Joey finally passed the other vehicle—then cut back in front of it and slammed on his brakes. The other car lost control trying to avoid a crash and went off the side of the road and down an embankment. Twenty-two year old Emmett Walsh had been ejected from his car (he hadn't been wearing a seatbelt) and died on the scene.

Joey had driven off. According to the report, he claimed he hadn't been aware there'd been a crash at all. Witnesses had given the police Joey's license plate number and he was initially charged only with driving with a suspended license (a previous DUI) but he was eventually charged with vehicular homicide.

Because Emmett's car hadn't actually made contact with Joey's, and because Emmett had also been driving recklessly, Joey was acquitted.

I wondered if this case had been tried in the present day and age if the verdict would be the same. It didn't make sense to me that Joey had gotten off scot-free since it had technically been his fault that the young man had to swerve because of Joey's actions...

Letting out a sigh, I closed the file. One thing was crystal clear after reading about Joey's many transgressions: He was a dirtbag. Scum. The lowest of the low. How he kept attracting women amazed me because just looking at his picture made me want to bathe in hand sanitizer.

I stuffed the file in my backpack and swept all the confetti bits back into a new envelope, sealed it, and placed it under my blotter.

Today was going to be a busy day, and the sooner I got started the better. I took another sip of coffee, finished up some paperwork, and headed out to meet my nursery supplier at Mario and Perry's.

In a little under an hour, the backyard makeover would be in full swing and hopefully it would run smoothly all day.

Because if it wasn't, I wouldn't be able to sneak over to the county offices to check out Cain Monahan...

And I couldn't let that happen. It was time to know the truth.

Chapter Eighteen

Back in the Mill, I parked my truck in my driveway and was happy to see most of my crew already gathered across the street. A Reaux Construction van was also parked over there. Apparently we weren't the only crew in town to get an early start.

I'd stopped on my way over to buy a new pair of work boots and to pick up some Krispy Kremes and plenty of coffee for the crew. I waved Marty Johnson over to distribute the goodies to my merry band of troublemakers as I affectionately called them.

I'd also brought some donuts home for Maria and Perry, but when I went into the house, I was surprised to find it empty. There was a note from Maria on the counter saying Nate had come by early to pick her up.

I felt a sudden stab of sadness and realized I'd miss her being here. Clearly I was losing my mind.

"Perry!" I called.

He wasn't due at the salon until ten, so I thought he'd still be around. I peeked out the kitchen window, wondering if he was across the street talking to Mario, but I didn't see either of them.

I was surprised by the little pang I felt at the house being empty. Usually I liked the peace and quiet, but I'd grown accustomed to Maria's demands over the past two days and Perry's theatrics.

And of course, the silence only reminded me again that Riley didn't live here anymore.

I really had to get a grip about that. It was silly. So silly. Even if he did live here, he'd be at school by now.

Dropping the donuts on the counter, I hitched myself onto a stool and opened my laptop for a quick search of my mail.

I lit up when I saw a note from my father.

And then deflated when I opened it.

Why do you want to know about The Black Fox?

I groaned and sent off a quick one-word note. *Curious.*

I logged off and had started to head back outside when I spotted something that did not belong here.

I crouched down.

Gracie wagged her tail from her spot beneath the couch.

Rubbing her ears, I said, "Who's a good girl?"

She closed her eyes and wagged faster.

Slowly, I stood, wincing at the way my knees made popping noises and went to the kitchen phone. I dialed Maria. She answered on the second ring.

"You forgot something here," I said.

"I did?"

She tried to sound innocent but I wasn't buying it.

"Maria," I warned.

"Nina, I don't really see what you're getting worked up about. Can't you just watch her for a week or two? Or a month? Just, you know, until the baby's home and settled in. Then we can introduce Gracie more smoothly."

"You're not serious."

"You don't like that plan?"

I noticed that Maria had left food and water bowls out for Gracie and both were topped off—I'm glad she remembered to do that, at least. "You need to come back and get her. I'll be out of the house all day."

"I can't, Nina. Nate's just left for work."

"I thought he was taking the week off?"

"I thought it was best that he get as much work done before the baby comes. He agreed."

I bet he did. "Then drive over here and get her yourself."

"I'm not sure that's a good idea. My blood pressure is a little high right now, so I need to lie down."

I bit the inside of my cheek. "What are you up to, Maria Ceceri Biederman?"

"I guess I could be persuaded to come by and get her if you also have my ultrasound results..."

Ah. Now I understood. "You're using your dog as a pawn? That's just low, Maria. Even for you."

"Don't use that tone with me, Nina. I'm desperate! And besides, we both know she likes you better than me."

"You're crazy."

"Take that back!"

"We also both know this is just some game you're playing because you're bored. You could easily go to the doctor's and get another ultrasound done instead of torturing me this way."

"Hmmph!" she said and hung up on me.

Gracie came out from beneath the couch and looked up at me with her cloudy eyes.

"I guess you're coming to work with me," I said.

If the piddle on the floor was any indication, she was as excited by the idea as I was.

***

Before I went to work, I stopped over at Mr. Cabrera's house to tell him about Brickhouse's travel plans. His car was in the driveway, but when I knocked and rang the doorbell, he didn't answer. I peered in the window, and the place looked deserted.

I hoped he wasn't hiding out. The big chicken.

Across the street, I tied Gracie to a maple tree in Mario and Perry's side yard, set out a water bowl, and laid out a towel for her in the shade. I found Kit in the back yard hard at work with the sod cutter, ripping up the sparse existing grass. The lawn had several varieties of grass seed and a poor root system.

It had to go. Yesterday, Coby had cut down two more diseased trees, and the change in the amount of sunshine now getting to the back yard was going to make all the difference with the new sod and plantings.

I glanced around at everyone hard at work. Coby and Marty had already started on building the new deck. Shay Oshwalter and Jeff Dannon were laying out a test paver pattern. It was going to take another hour or two before the yard was a clean slate—and then the work would really begin.

Kit shut down the sod cutter as I walked up to him.

"Where's Jean-Claude?" He should have been here by now.

"He called me this morning and said he'd be late. Delphine's due in court at nine and he wanted to be there. Plum's with him, too."

Delphine was still being charged with Joey's death.

I wondered if Honey would show up in court on Jean-Claude's arm. What a spectacle that would be.

I started thinking about Honey, and wondered again how she could have married Joey in the first place. She had to have sensed the sleaze factor.

"Why're you looking like that?" Kit asked. He wore a bandana wrapped around his bald head and safety eyewear.

No one dared make fun of him.

"Like what?" I asked.

"You know what."

I did know. I was meddling again. I needed to call Tam. It'd be nice to run a check on Honey, too.

187

I was starting to feel like I was getting in over my head, and that Kevin might be right—I should stay out of this.

But I was already in so far...a little more couldn't hurt.

I hoped.

Bear and Ethan came out on the back deck, lit their cigarettes, and looked around. I stepped closer to Kit. "How's it going in there?"

"Just about done," Kit said. "Plum called in an extra set of hands, a plumber, and that guy is finishing up in the basement. Between him and Bear and Ethan, the plumbing will be fixed today."

"So Mario will be moved back in tonight?"

"He better be."

I elbowed him. "You know you love him."

Kit eyed my elbow. I took a small step away from him.

"He wears smelly cologne, eats smelly cheese, and he snores."

"Louder than you?"

He stared. "Don't you have work to do?"

I did. "I need to make a call first." I started to walk away then turned back. "Did you happen to see Perry this morning? He was supposed to talk things over with Mario first thing today."

"I saw him."

"And?"

"He left again."

I wrinkled my nose. "Do you know where? Did they make up?"

"He stomped off, hopped in his car, and peeled out, so my guess is no. But I think Mario's just playing hard to get, especially after he went on and on about Perry last night at dinner. Made me sick."

"Right," I said. "Because you're made of stone."

"Something like that," he said.

"Right." I rocked on my heels. "When are you going to ask Ana to marry you, anyway?"

He snarled. "Go away."

"Just so you know, Saul has a nice selection of rings at The Gem Shop. Tell him I sent you and you can probably get the friends and family discount."

"Go. Away."

Smiling, I walked off, found a relatively quiet corner, and called Tam. At this rate, I was going to be babysitting Nic for a month straight.

As soon as I hung up with her, I called Perry. He didn't answer, and I left him a message that I'd called to check on him, and if he wanted to talk then to call me. I hoped Kit was right—that Mario was just playing hard to get at this point. He'd definitely been wronged by Perry, so I didn't blame him for putting Perry through the paces, but enough was enough.

I checked on Gracie, who was sound asleep under the tree, and wondered how long I could hold out until I ran over to the county offices.

Since they didn't even open 'til nine, I had two hours to kill by actually working.

It was going to be the longest two hours of my life.

Chapter Nineteen

Two hours later, I was itching to go. I glanced around and wiped the sweat off my brow.

The yard had come a long way in a short time. Heavy equipment like a skid steer loader helped speed the process along. The yard had been properly graded, new soil had been brought in using the bobcat and placed in the planting beds, and the preparation for the paver patio was almost complete.

To someone unfamiliar with the process of a makeover, it looked a complete mess. But I could easily see that we were right on schedule.

Jean-Claude still hadn't shown up, and I couldn't help but wonder how the hearing was going.

I walked over and checked on Gracie—she was still happily asleep. I thought for sure the vibrations from the equipment would startle her, but she was happily oblivious. All around her were the plantings the nursery had dropped off. I fingered one of the leaves of a star magnolia tree. It was past its bloom time now, but come next spring it would be beautiful. There were also two dogwoods as well as a beech tree to plant.

I bent down to check out the yellow flowers of the moonbeam coreopsis, and the tight buds on the wild blue indigo that would open in a few weeks. For a second, I was lost in the plants and the happiness they brought me. And for the first time in a long time I remembered why I loved my job so much.

A door slammed nearby and I glanced up just as Mr. Cabrera came out of his house and headed my way.

As soon as he spotted me, he tossed his hands in the air. "She's not answering my calls!"

"Can you blame her?"

A bushy eyebrow shot up. "Whose side are you on?"

"Both of yours. You need to go over there and talk to her. Don't do it on the phone. And you better hurry—she has a flight scheduled for tonight."

His face puckered, and he said, "Pah! I think I'll see if they need any help inside first." Turning, he walked away and went inside the house.

I wasn't sure what his "pah!" meant, but I had a feeling it wasn't good. My heart sank, but I realized that if he was going to get her back, he had to do the rest on his own. I'd helped him as much as I could.

I found Kit again and told him I needed to run an errand. I wasn't the least bit concerned leaving the yard under his control. Unfortunately, I couldn't leave Gracie under his watch. I brought her back to my house, settled her in the kitchen, safely behind a baby gate I used for her visits, and ran upstairs for a quick shower.

There was no way I was going to go see Cain Monahan while covered in a fine layer of dust and dirt.

I scrubbed the film from my skin and tried to tell myself that I hadn't completely lost my mind in seeking him out. But I knew I had. This was little more than a wild goose chase—and with a start I realized I was just as crazy as Maria. When we both had something stuck in our heads, it was hard to let it go.

For the millionth time since I met him, I silently thanked Perry for the easy-breezy haircut he'd given me. I combed through the wet strands and pulled out the hair dryer for a quick blow out. Tossing a look at my makeup bag, I debated whether a little mascara would make me look like I was trying too hard and decided I didn't care. I even dabbed on some lip gloss.

Sue me.

To prove that I wasn't fluffing myself up, as Mr. Cabrera would say, I threw on an old pair of jeans and a plain white T-shirt. I ran downstairs, said goodbye to Gracie, slipped on a pair of sandals and hopped in my truck.

It was closing in on eleven—it had taken me a while to get ready. I'd already let Ana know I was running late, but texted her now, too. *On my way.*

She texted back almost immediately. *I'll be on the lookout.*

With jittery hands, I put the truck in reverse and slowly backed out of my driveway. As I drove toward the county offices, I tried to shake the feeling that my life was about to change forever…

But I couldn't quite manage it.

***

Ana met me in the front lobby. "I did a little scoping out, and no one knows much about Cain Monahan. He's only been working here a few months."

"I have Tam on it," I said.

"Good, good. The coroner's offices are on the second floor. Do you want me to come with you?"

"I think I can do it on my own."

She studied me. "Are you wearing lip gloss?"

"Chapstick," I lied.

"My ass," she said.

"I'll check in with you when I'm done."

"I can hardly stand the suspense," she said, rubbing her hands.

I decided that my whole family had issues. Trying to calm my nerves with deep breathing, I took the stairs to the second floor. Harsh overhead lighting illuminated the wide hallway, and I was surprised at how luxurious the decor was from the thick rug to the dark wood wainscoting.

The county must be doing well for itself.

Small signs hung by each door in the hallway, and I stopped at the one that designated the coroner's office. My hand shook as I reached for the knob. I turned it and gave a little push.

There was no going back now.

The door opened into a small reception area, complete with four chairs, a coffee table, and a whole slew of magazines. A woman sitting behind a large wooden desk looked up when I came in.

"May I help you?"

"I'm here to see Cain Monahan."

She tapped on a keyboard. "Did you have an appointment?"

I tried not to fidget. "No, but he gave me his business card and told me to drop by any time if I had questions for him."

This was only a slight stretching of the truth— I was proud of myself.

"What is this in regard to?" she asked, looking me up and down and by the way her face turned stony, I barely passed muster.

I was glad I'd washed off the dirt or else she probably would have called security by now.

"The Joey Miller case," I said.

A look of recognition crossed her face. "I'm sorry, but Investigator Monahan isn't in the office right now. He's down in the morgue. Do you want to wait for him here?"

"Do you know how long he'll be?"

She shook her head. "Sorry."

Disappointment flooded me. "I'll come back later."

"Do you want to leave your name? I can have him call you and set up an appointment. That's the best way to reach him," she said snottily.

"Just tell him Nina Quinn stopped by."

She pasted on a fake smile. "Will do."

I left the office dragging my feet and trudged my way downstairs. Ana paced the lobby, her heels clicking on the marble floor. "He's in the morgue," I said.

Ana stared. "So?"

"So what? I didn't see him. And Ms. Snotty Pants doesn't know when he'll be back."

Ana placed her hands on my shoulders. "Nina, just go down there."

Panic sluiced through me. "Down where? The morgue?"

Eagerly, she nodded.

If I was the corpse whisperer, she was a corpse whisperer wannabe.

"You're out of your ever-loving mind. I am not going down there. There are dead people down there."

"Buck up! It's not as if you haven't seen dead people before. Up close and personal even."

She didn't need to remind me.

"Oh, come on," she said, grabbing my hand. "I'll go with you."

I allowed her to tug me along, only because I wanted to be done with this whole Cain Monahan mystery. To see the man's eyes, I'd risk seeing a few dead bodies.

Dread built in the pit of my stomach as we walked down the stairs. Ana talked on and on—about what I couldn't quite say. I'd tuned her out.

When she abruptly stopped in front of a door with MORGUE stenciled on a frosted glass pane, I started paying attention again.

"Do we knock?" I asked.

"I don't know," she said.

Before we could figure it out, the door opened and a man in scrubs came out, holding the door open for us. "Going in?" he asked.

I peeked inside and was relieved to see that it was some sort of anteroom with a desk, chairs, and a large opaque glass window. Not a toe tag to be seen.

Ana gave me a good shove. I didn't budge.

"Yes, we are," she said.

He eyed us. "Do you two need help?"

I couldn't find my voice.

"We're looking for Cain Monahan," Ana said.

"You just missed him. He was just called out on an emergency, not even five minutes ago. If you hurry, you might be able to catch him in the parking garage. Our spaces are on the first floor, north."

"Thanks!" Ana called and grabbed my arm. "I know a shortcut for employees only. This way."

She towed me along one corridor, then another. We zigged, we zagged, and finally she pushed open a heavy metal door leading into the garage.

We were both out of breath as we scanned the lot. Unfortunately, we'd made it out just in time to see Cain Monahan's taillights heading up the ramp toward the exit.

Ana swore. "I gave myself a blister for nothing."

Unexpected tears filled my eyes.

Ana swiped them away. "Try, try again, right?"

I nodded.

"Come on," she said, wrapping her arm around me. She swiped her badge to get back inside the building. "There's an ice cream stand just outside the lobby. How about a caramel sundae? It'll cheer you up."

"It's not even eleven in the morning."

"So?"

"I see your point. Okay."

As we walked, I received a text message from Tam. All it said was *Beware!*

"What's that about?" Ana asked.

"I'm not sure."

Almost immediately my phone rang. Maria. Ah. I understood Tam's message now. My sister was so transparent sometimes.

I answered with a light, "Hello?"

"*Neeeeee-naaaah!* How could you?"

"What?" I asked. Ana went on ahead to the ice cream cart, and I leaned against a light pole.

"You know what!"

"Look at it this way, Maria. You have something to occupy yourself until the baby's born."

She let out a small cry and hung up the phone.

Ana held out my sundae. "By the smile on your face you don't need this anymore."

I snatched it before she kept it for herself. "A little more cheer can't hurt."

I'd taken only one bite, however, when Ana said, "Uh oh."

I looked up to see Kevin running out of the building. He stopped short when he spotted us. I didn't like the look on his face. Not at all.

He bent at the waist and drew in a breath. "I've never been so happy to see you in all my life."

Ana shot me a worried glance.

"What's wrong?" I asked.

"What are you doing here?" he said. "Never mind! You need to come with me."

"Where?" I asked.

"Mario and Perry's house. There's been an accident. A horrible accident. I was at Delphine's hearing when the call came in."

Ana dropped her ice cream. "Who's hurt?"

His eyes softened. "I'm not sure. You can ride with us, too."

And just like that, I had the sick feeling that I knew where Cain Monahan had been heading...

Chapter Twenty

The ride to the Mill was nerve-wracking to say the least. With no details, my brain ran wild with various scenarios of what could have happened.

All of them bad.

There were any number of things that could go wrong on a job site. Having the heavy equipment around made the risk that much more.

Kevin had set lights on the dashboard and blared the siren. He drove as fast as the traffic allowed, his mouth set in a grim line. I glanced over my shoulder, into the backseat. An ashen pall had settled on Ana's skin as she stared out the window. Her hands were clenched in her lap.

My stomach roiled with anxiety.

If Cain Monahan had been called to the scene that meant someone was dead.

I closed my eyes and tried to scare up all the old prayers I'd learned at St. Valentine's. I silently pleaded that it not be true—that no one had been fatally injured. That Cain had been called somewhere else—anywhere else.

But as Kevin turned onto my street, I knew my pleas had been futile. The road was crowded with cars, including an ambulance that was screaming away from the scene. Three police cars and two fire trucks blocked the road. Parked directly in front of my house was a county coroner's car.

Ana rolled down the window and stuck her head out, her gaze zipping from face to face. "Do you see him?"

Kit.

"No," I said softly, still searching. "Not yet."

Kevin maneuvered the SUV onto the lawn of the house for sale as another ambulance pulled away, its lights flashing, its siren emitting a loud, "*Whoop, whoop!*"

He threw the car into park, shoved open the door, and started wading into the chaos.

Ana quickly hopped out, bobbing in between onlookers.

I sat, paralyzed.

What in the hell had happened?

Two ambulances? A death?

Next thing I knew, Kevin was at my side, tugging me out. "Come with me."

Numbly, I nodded and tried to mentally prepare for what I was about to see.

Kevin grabbed Ana's hand, too, as she weaved around the crowd, trying to find an opening.

"Police!" Kevin shouted loudly. "Move aside!"

It was a tone no one dared defy. The crowd parted just

enough for us to squeeze through. Kevin held up the yellow tape that had been roped around the yard to keep people at bay and Ana and I ducked under. He followed.

"Kit!" Ana cried. "Kit!"

The desperation in her voice cut straight to my soul. I swallowed hard, praying again. It was a jumbled prayer, a mix of what I remembered and silent begging.

Ana stood on tiptoes. "I don't see him. Kit!"

It was so loud here with the crowd and the emergency crews that I could barely hear her and she was standing next to me. If Kit was back there, mixed in with all the uniforms, then there was no way on earth he'd hear her either.

"Do you see him?" I asked Kevin.

His head moved left, then right, as he quickly scanned the yard, the faces. "Not yet."

Ana let out a cry and covered her mouth.

A commotion on the walkway caught my attention as another ambulance crew arrived. When I looked up at Kevin, he wore a stony expression, one I couldn't read.

Maybe I didn't want to read it.

"I'll be right back," he said and walked over to a uniformed officer who stood guard by the house's front door.

A movement near the tree where I'd tied Gracie earlier caught my eye. I squinted. Joy filled my heart as I grabbed Ana's arm. "There!"

A strangled sob came out of her mouth as she stumbled forward, first in an awkward walk, then in a full-out run. "Kit!"

Tears pooled in my eyes when he caught sight of her, and opened his arms wide to catch her as she launched herself at him. Her body pulsated as she sobbed into his chest. He clutched her tightly, rubbing her back and saying things into her ear. His gaze shifted to mine.

A teardrop spilled down my face as I nodded at him.

He nodded back.

I wanted to go over, get the details of what had happened, but didn't want to interrupt them. I did notice that Coby and Shay stood near Kit. But I didn't see Marty or Jeff.

The focus of what had happened seemed to be within the house, so I let out a small breath of relief that it hadn't involved my crew. That everyone was okay. But then I remembered that Mario and Mr. Cabrera had been in the house and some of Delphine's crew, too, and the anxiety started all over again.

I wrung my hands and watched Kevin as he finished his chat with the officer and came back to me.

"What happened?" I asked just as firefighters came out wearing fancy SCUBA-like ventilation gear.

"Carbon monoxide leak. Extremely high levels."

I sucked in a breath. I was about to ask if everyone was okay. But I knew by the coroner's vehicle that wasn't the case. "Who?" I said softly. "Who's hurt?"

"Mario, Mr. Cabrera, Ethan, and the plumber have been taken to the hospital. Bear is dead."

My bottom lip trembled. Tears filled my eyes again.

Kevin said, "Mario and the plumber are critical—they were with Bear in the basement where the leak originated. Mr. Cabrera and Ethan are stable—they were upstairs, working on tiling the bathroom. I can take you to the hospital."

My hand shook as I pulled out my cell phone. "I need to call Perry."

He nodded.

As I tried to dial, my fingers kept slipping off the numbers. Kit and Ana walked up to us, and she clung to him like a barnacle to a rock. I gave Kit a quick hug and said, "I have to call Perry and Brickhouse."

"Already did," Kit said. "Neither answered."

I swore under my breath.

"I'll send a car to the salon and to Brickhouse's townhouse," Kevin said. "You ready to go?"

"We're going to the hospital," I said. "Did you two want to come?"

Kit shook his head. "I'll stay here and wrap up the job for the day. Everyone's pretty shaken up knowing that we were all just outside while that was going on inside."

"Who found them?" I asked, rubbing my temples. I couldn't believe the turn this day had taken.

"Mr. Cabrera came outside for some fresh air after feeling woozy and passed out. I called for help and went inside to see if everyone else was okay... They weren't."

Ana sniffled and clung a little tighter.

"We should go," Kevin said, putting his arm around me.

I leaned into him, grateful for the support, and said, "Ana, can you check on Gracie in a little while? She's in my kitchen."

She nodded.

"Kit, tell the crew... Tell them I'll email later."

"Will do."

As Kevin and I threaded through the crowd, I checked to see if the coroner's car was still there, but it was gone.

Kevin used his lights and sirens to get me to the hospital in no time flat. We hadn't said a word to each other the whole ride. As he pulled up in front of the emergency room drop-off he finally said, "You'll be okay on your own?"

"You're leaving?"

His eyes looked troubled. "I need to get back to the scene."

"Why?" He was a homicide detective. "This was just a horrible accident. Wasn't it?"

"The fire department doesn't think so, Nina. It looks like someone tampered with the water heater. This case is a homicide investigation."

***

I had a hell of a time getting any information at the hospital. I finally had to lie and say I was Mr. Cabrera's daughter and Mario's cousin so the nurse would tell me anything about their conditions.

Mr. Cabrera and Ethan had been lucky—they'd been

working in the bathroom with the window open. They were being treated—as were all the others—in hyperbaric oxygen chambers to increase the oxygen flow that the carbon monoxide had robbed from them.

There was a good chance for a full recovery for the two of them. Mario's and the plumber's conditions were still critical, as they were both still unconscious. The doctors feared the likelihood of brain damage for both of them due to lack of oxygen.

I paced the hospital's ICU hallway, passing the plumber's family, who sat stunned in the waiting area. I'd just completed another loop when the elevator doors opened and Perry flew out with an officer I recognized following behind him.

I'd never seen Perry look so...undone. His hair stuck up, his eyes held a wild beastly look, and I could tell by the puffiness around his eyes that he'd been crying.

He ran over to me. "Where is he? How is he?"

I explained about the treatment. "You need to talk to his doctor." I didn't want to be the one to tell him about the possible side effects.

"Who?" he asked.

"Dr. Kopec. Check with the desk." He started off and I grabbed his arm. "If anyone asks, I'm Mario's cousin and Mr. Cabrera's daughter."

Dazed, he nodded, and headed for the nurses' station.

The officer, Doug Keegan, looked at me. "He'll be okay here with you, Nina?"

I nodded. "Did you drive him over?"

Doug was a nice guy, married to Lindsey, a girl I went to high school with—and also a client of Perry's. "Yeah. We had to stop at his house first for medical paperwork. He was scared the doctor wouldn't let him see Mario without it. Then the FD wouldn't let him in the house... It was an ordeal until Kevin stepped in."

Kevin had not only stepped in today, but he'd stepped up. I thought of the way he'd taken Ana's hand when we first arrived at Mario and Perry's house... Taking care of her without even thinking twice about it.

Taking care of me.

"Well, I can take it from here," I said.

He tipped his hat and started to walk away.

"Doug?" I called. He turned. "Has there been any luck finding Ursula Krauss?"

"She wasn't home."

"Thanks for trying."

At the end of the hall, I spotted Perry talking with Dr. Kopec. Undoubtedly, he was hearing the same news about brain damage and heart function.

Anger slowly built in my chest. How could someone have done this on purpose? Why?

I thought back to the day before when I saw Bear and Ethan installing the water heater. Anyone could have tampered with it between then and this morning. The house wasn't exactly Fort Knox—I could probably pick the lock on the back slider.

I thought about Plum and how she'd been the only crew not working today...and wondered how her talk with Bear had gone. Because if it hadn't gone well, maybe she would have wanted him dead.

But why risk everyone else's lives?

I needed to let Kevin know about Plum and her fixation with Bear. I'd forgotten all about it while I was with him. But making a phone call meant having to leave Perry here alone. Something I couldn't do quite yet.

Perry slowly walked back to me with such a despairing look in his eyes that my heart broke all over again. I led him over to a chair and had him sit down.

"He's strong," I said. "And stubborn. He'll pull through."

Perry stared at a spot on the floor.

I sat down next to him and just held his hand for a while.

After ten minutes or so, he said, "How're the others?"

"Mr. Cabrera and Ethan are stable and expected to recover. The plumber Plum had called in to help is the same as Mario. You heard about Bear?"

Nodding, he said, "He was a nice guy. A little rough around the edges but a nice guy."

I recalled his advice yesterday to Mario. "Yeah, he seemed to be."

I didn't mention my suspicion that he might have killed Joey.

We sat in silence for a little bit longer and stiffened when Dr. Kopec walked into the waiting room. He walked by us and headed toward the family of the plumber, asking to speak with them in a conference room down the hallway.

Perry squeezed my hand so tight I thought for sure bones would break, but I didn't let go of his hand or try to wiggle away.

An older woman shook her head fiercely and held onto a young boy's hand much like Perry was holding on to mine. "Just tell us," she said.

The doctor crouched down. "I'm very sorry to tell you he didn't make it. I'm so sorry."

The woman's eyes opened wide and stayed that way until a chaplain came into the room a minute later. When she saw the man of the cloth, she broke down, crumpling to the floor.

I glanced at Perry. "Let's go for a walk."

Tears shimmered in his eyes. "Okay."

I jabbed the elevator button as the woman's cries echoed down the hallway, and when the doors opened, I leaped inside and jabbed the button for the first floor as though my life depended on it.

Perry slumped in a corner of the elevator, and I said angrily, "He's strong, damn it!"

His head snapped up, and his eyes were a watery mess. He wiped his nose with the back of his hand, lifted his chin, and said, "Damn right!"

We both pretended not to hear the way his voice cracked when he said it.

Outside, the sun was shining and birds chattered as though

nothing life-altering was happening within the walls just beyond the trees where they nested. I took a few deep breaths, breathing in the clean spring air, and trying to breathe out my anxiety, fear, and worry.

Perry sat on a bench, turned his face upward to the sun and closed his eyes. His lips moved, saying over and over again, "He's strong, he's strong, he's strong."

My cell phone rang as I paced the sidewalk. Tam.

"Nina, thank goodness. Kit filled me in on everything. How's Mr. Cabrera. How's Mario?"

"No change yet," I said.

There was quiet on the line, then a sniffle. "I just can't believe this. Is Ursula there yet?"

"Not yet. No one's been able to reach her. She's not answering her phone, and she's not at home."

"Has anyone tried calling Claudia?"

Claudia, Brickhouse's daughter. "I didn't even think about it."

"I can do that."

"Thanks, Tam."

"I had another reason for calling," she said, her tone not quite right.

"Why's that?"

"I've been doing that extra work for you, you know."

"I know."

"And well, the fingerprint stuff takes a while. It's not like

211

you see on TV."

I knew that. I didn't expect any news for a couple of days.

"But," she said, "I found Honey Miller's information easily."

"And," I said, feeling my anxiety rising again.

"Did you read the full report on Joey Miller this morning? Did you see that vehicular homicide charge he was acquitted of?"

"Yes..."

"Well, turns out that Honey Walsh Miller was the victim's younger sister. She was twelve when Emmett Walsh died. I don't think it's just a coincidence that she married the man who'd been accused of killing her brother. Do you?"

My heart thrummed. "You know how I feel about coincidences. I need to call Kevin."

"If you could leave my name out of it...," she said meekly.

"I will. Thanks, Tam. You're amazing."

I hung up and glanced over at Perry. He still had his face toward the sun, still mouthing a silent mantra.

I dialed Kevin. He didn't answer. I left a message saying I needed to speak to him right away, that it was urgent, and so help me he would regret it if he didn't call me as soon as he got this message.

I'd just tucked my phone in my pocket when I turned and saw Cain Monahan striding up to the hospital doors. He spotted me and altered his course, heading straight toward me.

I cursed my luck that the man had his sunglasses on again.

"How're your friends?" he asked as he neared.

I didn't question how he'd known they were my friends. I had an eerie feeling that he knew much more about me than I did him.

I tried not to stare at his scars as I said, "The same. The other man, the plumber, didn't make it."

I hated that I didn't know the man's name. But sure as I stood there, I would never forget his wife's grief.

"I know," he said. "That's why I'm here."

"Ah," I said, feeling foolish for not putting that together.

"I heard you stopped by my office this morning."

It seemed like forever ago.

"You had a question for me?"

In light of everything, my wild goose chase felt incredibly silly. Indulgent. I shrugged. "It wasn't a big deal," I lied.

He tipped his head to the side. My throat closed a little. Seth used to do the same. Then I told myself that lots of people did that. Even so, I couldn't help but ask, "Did I see you at the park the other day?"

"Maybe," he said evasively. "I'm there a lot."

"Running?"

He nodded.

"Did you run cross country in high school?"

He did the head-tipping thing again. "Why do you ask?"

"Curious." My heart was pounding now, my pulse throbbing in my ears.

"Look, Ms. Quinn."

"Nina, please."

"Nina." He suddenly frowned, then said my name again. "Nina..."

"What?"

"Nothing."

"It's something."

"It's stupid." He grimaced. "I just...for some reason..."

"What?" I pressed.

He laughed this time, and I felt light-headed. He'd laughed Seth's laugh.

He said, "I just had the biggest urge to say Nina Bo-bina. And I'm sorry, that's really stupid."

I swayed a little. Nina Bo-bina was a childhood nickname given to me by my brother. All his friends used to call me Bo-bina.

Reaching out, he grabbed onto my arm to steady me. "Are you okay?"

"Take off your sunglasses."

"Pardon?"

"Please take off your sunglasses."

He held onto me with one arm, and with the other, he slowly reached up and took off his glasses.

Suddenly, I didn't want to see. I didn't want to know. I slammed my eyes shut.

"Nina?"

His voice questioned, but there was something else there... A quiet plea. He wanted me to look. And that was all the invitation I needed.

I cracked open one eye, then the other, and slowly lifted my head to look him in the eyes.

He searched my face, seemingly looking for answers to his own questions, and my knees went weak with what I saw.

The confusion. The doubt. The hint of fear. The milk chocolate brown irises dotted with flecks of gold.

Feeling woozy, I could barely force the name from my lips. "Seth."

And almost as though that effort had been too much, my body went slack, and my world went dark.

Chapter Twenty-one

I woke up in a hospital bed with Kevin hovering over me, kissing my face.

"Stop that!" a voice from across the room said. "She's not Snow White, and you're making me sick."

Maria.

I popped open an eye and squinted. The room was bright, and I wished I'd kept my eyes closed because suddenly my head throbbed like my skull had been cracked open. "What happened?"

Maria appeared at my bedside. "You cracked your skull open!"

"What?"

Kevin held my hand. "It's not that bad. You fainted and hit your head on the sidewalk. The doctor says it's a concussion. You've been in and out of it for a few hours now."

Fainted.

Seth.

I struggled to sit up, but Kevin pushed me back down. He said, "The doctor said no sudden movements."

I stared at him. "Were you *kissing* me?"

His jaw twitched. "You don't have to make it sound like it's a bad thing."

I wasn't sure it was a *good* thing.

"Plus," he added, "it always works in the movies."

I flicked my gaze to Maria. "Mr. Cabrera? Mario?"

She smoothed the hospital blankets. "Mr. Cabrera's awake and talking. The doctors want to keep him for observation tonight and he can likely go home tomorrow. Kit and Ana are up with him."

"No Brickhouse?"

Maria said, "Tam called Claudia who told her that Ursula had taken an earlier flight. We're trying to track her down in Florida."

"Mario?"

"He's a little bit better. Still getting oxygen treatments."

"Is he awake?"

"Not yet," Maria said. "Perry's with him."

"Ethan?"

"Same story as Mr. Cabrera," Kevin said.

I closed my eyes and fought against the pain. My thoughts swirled, one taking precedence over the others.

Why was Seth Thiessen pretending to be another man?

"Looks like she's out again," Kevin whispered.

"No," I mumbled. "I'm just thinking."

"Do you remember why you called me?" he asked. "You said it was urgent."

Honey! I tried to sit up again, but he kept pushing me down. "Stop that!" I ordered. He held his hands up in surrender, and I struggled into a sitting position. "I, um, learned some information about Honey Miller."

Kevin's hands curled around the bed's guardrail.

"And there's something you should know about Plum, too," I added.

"Nina," he warned.

I groaned and held my head.

He rolled his eyes, not buying my act.

It had been worth a try. "Just let me say it and you can yell at me later, okay?"

"Fine. Spill."

I winced in pain—real this time. Maybe sitting up hadn't been a good idea. I scooted back down. "Long story short, Honey Miller is the sister of a man killed in Michigan ten years ago. Joey had been charged in his death."

Kevin didn't so much as blink, but Maria said, "Shut the front door!"

"And Plum?" he finally said through clenched teeth.

"Is—was—in love with Bear. She supposedly was going to talk with him yesterday about her feelings. I don't know if the conversation took place, but if it did and it didn't go well..."

Kevin let loose a string of curse words. "I've got to go." He looked at Maria. "You'll take care of her?"

"We have it covered," she said, motioning to her big belly.

Kevin headed for the door, then stopped abruptly. "By the way, Perry said you were speaking with a man he didn't recognize when you fainted. Who was it?"

I debated lying but finally said, "Cain Monahan."

"The coroner's investigator?"

Maria said, "Hubba hubba!"

I shot her a now's-not-the-time-look.

Kevin's eyes flashed greener than usual. "I see."

He didn't, but I wasn't in the mood to argue.

"I'll check on you later," he said and stormed out the door.

Maria pulled a chair over to the bed. "Someone's worked up and more than a little jealous." She leaned on the bed and waggled her eyebrows. "Any reason for him to be?"

"I saw his eyes, Maria," I said quietly.

She straightened. "And?"

"It's him."

"But why... How? He's...dead."

"He's clearly not. And I don't know the whys and hows of it all. But I'm determined to find out."

***

Early the next morning, I was camped out on my sofa with

Gracie tucked in next to my ankles, and my laptop balanced precariously on my lap.

I'd been released from the hospital late last night only after Maria promised the doctor she'd stay with me all night long.

Which explained why she was snuggled up in the recliner, wrapped in an afghan and sound asleep.

I smiled thinking about her, and how she'd mother-henned me all night long. She was going to be a good mama.

Before I'd left the hospital, I'd checked on both Mario and Mr. Cabrera. Mr. Cabrera had seemed depressed, and the doctor said that was a common side effect of carbon monoxide poisoning, but I wondered if it had more to do with Brickhouse's absence.

Maria and I had promised him that we'd come back and pick him up as soon as he was sprung.

Perry had been asleep in Mario's room, but Mario had been undergoing more tests. I tucked a note into Perry's shirt pocket and was just waiting for the sun to come up a little bit more before I called to get an update.

I logged on to my computer, and checked my email. My father had written back. *Your mother wants me to tell you curiosity and cats, Nina.*

I frowned at the screen. *Hmmph.* I couldn't quite understand why he wasn't spilling everything he knew. I almost wrote back that Seth Thiessen was alive and that's why I was curious, but I didn't dare. I wanted to figure out why he was pretending to be someone else first.

Tam had sent me an email with three attachments. One for Ethan, Bear, and Honey.

I clicked open Ethan's file first and was shocked beyond reason to see that he had a clean record. He was twenty-three, had grown up and gone to school in Indiana, graduated from a well-known college with a theater degree of all things, and had only lived in Cincinnati a few months.

I would've sworn he belonged on the FBI's most wanted list. I guess that showed just how good my instincts were.

With a tinge of sadness, I opened Bear's folder. He was thirty—my age—and had a rap sheet a mile long. Mostly petty stuff with some assaults thrown in for good measure.

I'd saved Honey's for last, hoping to devote more time to it. But as soon as I opened the file, I was quickly distracted by the articles Tam had found about Honey's brother's death. I barely registered Honey's age, her schooling, her lack of an arrest record. My gaze kept jumping to the photos of a tearful family and a young girl who'd lost her only brother much too young.

On one hand, my heart broke for her. On the other, I suspected she married Joey to seek revenge.

The question remained if she had found it.

Kevin had, in fact, checked in on me last night, but he'd been cold and distant, and I'd felt guilty for half a second for keeping the whole Seth thing to myself, but then decided to let the guilt go. There was too much other stuff going on. I'd given no reason for Kevin to act the way he was, and he was just going to have to get over himself.

Kevin had come bearing the news that both Bear and the plumber both had enlarged hearts and that had contributed to their deaths. Weakened systems were easily susceptible to carbon monoxide poisoning.

I kept telling myself that Mario was strong. He was young and strong. He would pull through. For Perry's sake, he had to.

Kevin said nothing about Honey or Plum or their possible link to the recent crime spree in the neighborhood.

My head snapped up when I heard a car door slam out front. I craned my neck to see who it was, but couldn't see through the curtain sheers in the dim morning light. Who on earth would show up at six thirty in the morning?

A key slid into the front door lock, and I watched the doorknob turn. I'd have gotten up, just in case someone was breaking in, but my head hurt too badly when I moved. If it was a killer out to get me, I was a goner.

The door creaked open, and I glanced at Gracie snoring away. Sometimes I envied her life.

A head popped through the doorway, and I relaxed and set my laptop on the coffee table.

"Hey," Riley said softly. "I was hoping you'd be up."

I was always up early, it seemed. Even when concussed and wanting to sleep for a week straight. My heart melted a bit that he'd stopped by on his way to school.

He held up a bag as he walked past me into the kitchen. Quietly, he said, "I brought you some donuts. How's your head?"

"It's fine," I whispered.

"Sure it is. Hey, you already have donuts here."

"Yeah, but they're a day old. I was planning to let Maria have them."

She cracked open an eye. "I heard that."

"You want a glazed or a lemon-filled?" he asked.

"Glazed," I said.

"Both." Maria yawned and then rubbed her belly. "Baby's hungry."

Riley brought plates out to us and sat on the coffee table. He stared at me. "You don't look too bad."

"Thanks," I said dryly.

He squinted. "Is that mascara smudging your face? Why were you wearing makeup?"

I wiped my eyes. "A moment of insanity."

"You're okay, though?"

I bit into the donut. It was still hot, and I think I moaned a little. I tried to ease his worry. "I'll be fine in a day or two."

"Okay. Good. I can come by after school and stay with you. Dad said you couldn't be alone."

"Hey," Maria said. "I'm sitting right here."

He smiled. "In case Aunt Maria wants to go back home."

"Oh no," she said. "I'm here for a few days, at least. I already told Nate."

She was serious. Oh no. No, no, no. "Maria, you don't have

to..."

She pouted—her lips were covered in powdered sugar. "My house is so boring. This place is much more exciting."

I tried to hide my dismay. There was no way I was getting rid of her. "You can still come by after school, Ry."

"Maybe." Standing, he walked toward the door. "I've got to get to school."

"Hey," I said, waving him toward me. "Come back here."

He stood behind the couch.

I smiled. "Lower, lower..." He bent down, allowing me to kiss the top of his head. "Thanks for the donuts."

"It was nothing," he said. "I'll see you later."

The door slammed shut and Gracie lifted her head, looked around, and then went back to sleep.

"That kid's all right," Maria said.

"Yeah, he is." I smiled and scooted back down into my covers, closing my eyes.

Something was bothering me, some tidbit just outside my reach. I blamed the concussion and lack of sleep. Hopefully it would come back to me.

"Tomorrow, though," she said, "I'll see if he can bring us chocolate donuts. I could really go for some chocolate right now."

"There are some in the day-old donut box."

There was a beat of silence, and I opened an eye to find her staring longingly into the kitchen.

She caught me watching her. "I don't eat day-old donuts, Nina. That's...that's..."

"Delicious? They're not moldy or anything. There are some plain chocolate, some chocolate-filled, and some chocolate frosted ones with sprinkles."

Her eyebrows had gone up, and she was practically salivating. She finagled her way out of the recliner. "I meant to say that I don't eat day-old donuts except for today. Today I'll make an exception."

"I thought you might change your mind."

Her voice carried from the kitchen. "You won't tell anyone, right?"

I smiled. "My lips are sealed, Maria."

"Nina?"

"Yeah?"

"Were you expecting Tam and Ian to show up this morning?"

"No, why?"

"They just pulled in your driveway."

Wincing, I sat up. Maria wiped chocolate crumbs off her face as she waddled to the door and opened it before they could even knock.

"Sorry to barge in like this," Tam said as Ian followed her into the house.

I looked between their faces. Tam was clearly worried, and Ian wore a grim expression. "What's wrong? Is it Mario?"

"No, no," Tam said, sitting in the armchair next to the couch. Ian sat on its foot stool. "He's fine."

"Then why are you here?" I asked, feeling slightly sick to my stomach.

Tam glanced at me, then at Ian. "We have a problem. A big, big problem."

Chapter Twenty-two

"It's like this," Tam said, taking a deep breath. "I sent you the reports on Ethan, Honey, and Bear..."

"Right."

"But not Cain Monahan," Tam said. She looked at Ian. "There was nothing on file for him, except for his prints because he's a government employee. I couldn't find anything much. He's thirty-four, not married, graduated from the University of Florida." She trailed off.

"Then what's the problem?" I asked.

"You opened a hornet's nest, Nina," Ian said. I'd met him last year while he'd been working undercover for the FBI. He'd since switched to the DEA.

"How so?" I was trying to remember how to breathe properly. They were making me nervous.

"Tam's Internet search spurred a visit by the U.S. Marshals to our farm," he said.

Pain pulsated in my head. "I don't understand."

Maria settled herself back into the recliner. "Me, either."

"I didn't either," Tam said, "until they explained."

"Let's backtrack a little. Why did you want to know about Cain Monahan?" he asked.

I didn't want to backtrack. I bit the inside of my cheek. "Personal reasons."

"Personal why?" he asked.

"Why does it matter?" I winced at my headache.

"Just tell him, Nina," Maria said.

Ian watched me closely. "Fine," I said. "I met Cain the other day when he was here working the Joey Miller case. I was a little taken aback because he reminded me of someone I used to know. Someone who's dead. The thing is, I know it's him. I know it is. I saw his eyes... But Cain is not his name."

Ian nodded, not seeming the least bit surprised. "His name is Seth Thiessen."

My jaw dropped.

"Holy shit!" Maria clapped a hand over her mouth. Through her fingers, she said, "I thought you were just crazy, Nina."

"Thanks," I said to her.

"Sorry." She shrugged.

Ian said, "Do you know any of the duties of the U.S. Marshals?"

"Not really," I said.

He clasped his hands together and leaned forward. "Well, one of the many duties is the Witness Protection program."

I let his words sink in. Realization hit me hard. "The plane crash." Now it made sense why there had been no follow up.

"Exactly," Ian said. "No one was on that plane—it was a ruse. The family was relocated to Florida to start a new life."

"But his scars..."

"There was another accident, a car accident in Florida. His family died, and he was in a coma for months."

"That's...horrible. Did the Witness Protection fail them?" Maria asked.

"Actually, no," Ian said. "It was just an accident. A tragic accident. Seth finally came to, but had little memory of who he used to be. A blessing, I guess, considering. He truly started a new life."

No wonder he hadn't recognized me right off. He wasn't pretending to be someone else. He *was* someone else. I thought of his parents and his sister, and my heart ached.

"He was taken in and adopted by a Marshal in Florida," Ian said, "where he finished high school and went to college."

Maria leaned forward, which wasn't easy for her to do. "If he has no memories of his childhood, what's he doing here?"

I was struggling to wrap my head around all this. "When I was talking to him yesterday, he said he wanted to call me Bobina."

Maria gasped.

"It was a childhood nickname he used to call me," I explained to Tam and Ian. "So he must remember some stuff."

"It's definitely possible. It turns out his adopted father, the only family he knew after the accident, died last year, and shortly afterward Cain moved back to Ohio. Before he died, his adopted father expressed concern to his colleagues that Cain would eventually investigate his childhood. The father feared that even twenty years later that there might still be some bad blood toward the Thiessen family. The Marshals were put on alert when Cain moved. Then when Tam started searching...they paid us a visit. Who else knows you were looking into his background?"

"Just Maria. And Ana, but she wouldn't say anything."

"Good. I was asked to convey to you that you need to keep quiet about all this until it's ascertained whether there remains a viable threat to Cain's life. It's doubtful, but the Marshals are checking with the FBI, and there are hoops to jump through. So...until you hear from me, mum's the word."

"Our lips are sealed. Right, Nina?" Maria said.

Seth was alive. He was alive! I couldn't wait to tell Peter. But, I'd wait. I couldn't do anything to jeopardize putting Seth in danger again. "Sealed," I agreed.

"Good." Ian stood up.

Behind him Tam gave me a thumb's up.

"Oh, and by the way," he said, "Tam's fingerprinting service is closed for good. You should have seen me trying to double-talk my way out of trouble yesterday."

Tam frowned and gave me a thumbs down.

"Does that mean I don't have to babysit for those hours?"

He laughed. "On the contrary—your hours have doubled."

"That hardly seems fair," I said.

"Would you like me to send the Marshals here for an interview?"

"Doubled it is!"

Tam kissed me on the head before they headed out. "Call me if you get an update from the hospital."

"I will," I promised.

The door closed softly behind them. I glanced at Maria.

Her blond hair shimmered as she said, "Can you even believe it?"

I leaned back on my pillow and smiled. "I can. I saw his eyes." A second later, I heard hammering. "Is that in my head or outside?"

She wiggled out of the chair and went to the window. "Oh my word. You have to see this."

***

Squinting against the pain in my head, I was careful not to disturb Gracie as I stood up and went to the window. Pulling aside the curtain, I peeked out.

Dozens of scary-looking people milled about along with some familiar faces. The sound of a circular saw split the air, and I saw a man decked out in tattoos and leather bringing a piece of trim work into Mario and Perry's house.

"What in the world?" I grabbed my robe, tied the sash, and stepped out onto the front porch. Ana, dressed in a pair of cut-off shorts, tank, and pink tool belt was headed my way.

"Do you have any good coffee?" she asked. "Kit's stuff is too weak, and I don't have the heart to tell him."

"In the kitchen. What's going on?"

She smiled and it lit her whole face. "Kit called in a few friends to finish Mario and Perry's house for good."

"Who?" Maria asked. "The Hell's Angels?"

A dozen motorcycles—at least—were parked in Kit's front yard.

"I don't ask questions like that," Ana said, ducking past me. She was back a second later with a mug of coffee.

"Why is my crew there?" I'd emailed them last night, telling them to enjoy the day off today and we'd pick up on Mario and Perry's yard on Wednesday or Thursday (Tuesday was our regular day off) once we all got our bearings again.

"Kit heard there was rain in the forecast for tonight and called to see if anyone would come in today. Everyone agreed. Plus, I think after what happened, they want to get it done for Mario and Perry."

"Aw," Maria said.

I felt the sting of tears and blinked them back.

"I took the day off to help. A mental health day. After yesterday's trauma, I need it."

I didn't crack any jokes about her renovation skill level. For Kit to do all this—and for people to show up—it restored my faith in humanity.

"Kit says not to worry about anything. That he has things covered and for you to rest."

"Tell him I said thanks. For everything."

Nodding, she waved as she walked off, and earned several catcalls from men pulling up on their Harleys.

Maria said, "I think I saw that guy on a Wanted poster once."

I smiled. "He's winking at you."

"Eee!" she cried and ducked back into the house.

I stood outside for a moment, taking in the sight of dozens of strangers pitching in to help two men they didn't know. It did my heart good.

Really good.

Chapter Twenty-three

The day only improved when we swung by the hospital. We were there to pick up Mr. Cabrera, but we'd gone upstairs to check on Mario first and found that they'd moved him to a private room. When we walked in, he was sitting up in bed looking a little ragged but none the worse for wear.

"Mario, look at you!"

He smiled weakly. Maria and I took turns kissing his cheek.

Perry yawned and said, "Isn't it great? He woke up in the middle of the night. The doctor says he's not quite out of the woods yet, but he's getting there. The worst is past."

I went to hold Mario's hand and found it shaking. "Are you cold? I can get another blanket."

"It's a side effect," he said softly, his voice scratchy.

Perry said, "He'll probably need some physical therapy when he's released."

"Big!" Mario said, eyeing Maria's stomach.

She shook a finger at him and said, "I'll forgive you for saying that only because of what happened."

Confusion flooded his eyes. "What happened?"

I glanced at Perry.

"There are some memory issues, too. There was an accident," Perry explained patiently to him.

Mario nodded and closed his eyes.

Perry motioned us out of the room.

"Memory issues?" I said. "Will they last?"

"I hope so!" Perry said.

Maria stared at him. "Perry Owens, are you insane?"

"Not at all. Right now he doesn't remember our fight at all. He's not mad at me, and I'd like to keep it that way. It's like a clean slate."

I couldn't help but shake my head. "You're awful."

Maria said, "I'll be right back," and veered off toward a restroom.

"When's she due?" Perry asked.

"The induction is at the end of next week."

"She looks ready to pop."

"Well, if you value your life, then don't tell her that."

He glanced back into the room. "He'll be out for a little while now, can I catch a ride with you two? I'd like to take a shower and freshen up a little."

"Sure," I said. "We were just headed downstairs to collect Mr. Cabrera."

"Any sign of Brickhouse?"

I shook my head.

He whistled low. "Let me just tell the nurses where I'm

going. I'll be right back."

I leaned against the door frame, watching Mario sleep. I supposed if he came out of this missing a week's worth of bad memories and a slight tremor then he was one lucky man.

Perry came back and nudged me. "What're you thinking about? You look lost in thought."

"Just how lucky he was," I said.

"No," Perry said softly. "I was the lucky one."

***

We'd explained to Perry about the goings-on at his house during the ride home so he wouldn't be taken aback by the motorcycle gang that had shown up in his yard.

He had tears in his eyes as we pulled into my driveway.

Mr. Cabrera looked as sullen as the storm clouds on the horizon. I said, "Maybe you should stay with me for a few days, Mr. C."

"Pah," he said. "I'd rather go home."

Maria said, "No, really, stay with us."

"Us?" he echoed.

"Maria's staying with me for a couple of days."

She said, "On account that Nina cracked her head open yesterday and needs someone looking after her."

He stared at my head. "Doesn't look like anything's wrong with your head."

I said, "Only on the inside."

A smile tugged the corner of his lip. "That makes more sense." He pushed open the car door. "But all the same, I'd rather go home."

"Dinner at least," I offered.

Reluctantly, he nodded and toddled away. I made a mental note to check on him later.

Perry helped Maria out of the car. "Have you heard from Kevin at all today?" he asked me.

"Not a thing." I headed for the front steps.

Maria carefully navigated the stairs. "He's mad at her because he thinks she has a thing for the coroner guy."

Perry said, "Do tell!"

"Nothing to tell." There was a package sitting on my welcome mat. "Do *you* have something to tell?"

"Oh no, that's not from me," he said. "I learned that lesson."

I bent down, cursing the pain and pressure in my head, and straightened back up. "The tag has your name on it."

He took the box out of my hands and shook it. "Impossible."

"Open it," Maria said.

Perry tore open the wrapping and removed a small velvet box from inside a larger gift box. The hinges creaked slightly when he pulled back the top. "I don't understand," he said.

"What is it?" Maria leaned in, trying to see the gift.

I glanced at Perry. "Come on, you're behind this."

He shoved the box into my hands. "I'm not. I swear I'm not. I don't get it. Who'd send me these?"

In my hands were the cufflinks he'd admired the other day at The Gem Shop.

"You really didn't send them to yourself?" I asked.

"Nina, I'm telling you, no. I learned my lesson. This is a little creepy, isn't it?"

"Why don't we call Saul?" I said.

A quick phone call later, we were still stumped. Saul had cited store policy about revealing his customers' names and hung up.

Maria looked at me. "This is strange."

"Definitely a little creepy," I said.

Perry eyed the cufflinks. "Do you think I can keep them? I can tell Mario he gave them to me—he won't remember."

I snatched the box back. "No!"

"I knew you were going to say that." He marched upstairs to take a shower.

As I watched Gracie sniff around outside, I shifted the box from hand to hand.

"What are you going to do with them?" Maria asked.

"I think I need to pay Saul a visit." I brought Gracie back inside, rubbed her head, and set her on her favorite spot under the couch. "Do you want to come along?"

"Actually, I'm a little tired. I think I'll rest a bit."

I eyed her. "Is *Small-Town Crown* coming on TV soon?"

"At two!"

I smiled, but her staying here posed a problem. I couldn't go alone because I wasn't yet cleared to drive. "I'll see if Ana will go."

"Can you bring me home a shake? Since you're going out? A chocolate one?"

As I walked out the door, I figured a lot of things about Maria were about to undergo a drastic change. And some things would forever stay the same.

Chapter Twenty-four

I'd just stepped outside when Kevin pulled his SUV behind Maria's Mercedes.

"I thought you were supposed to be resting," he said.

"I've rested. Now I have a quick errand to run."

"You're not driving..."

"I was going to get Ana to take me." Across the street, she was passing out water bottles to Kit's scary-looking friends. I noticed Jean-Claude was hard at work, stacking shrubs into a wheelbarrow. I hadn't spoken with him since the day at the park. I hoped he was okay—there was a lot going on in his life. I saw that several neighbors had joined in the cause to fix up the house as well, and also hoped Mario and Perry realized how welcomed they were here.

"She appears to be busy. I'll take you."

"You don't even know where I'm going."

His gaze settled on me. "Doesn't matter."

Warmth slid down my spine. "Okay."

He held my hand as I settled into the passenger seat, and I wondered at the shift in his behavior. He'd gone from being surly to being...flirty?

"Where to?" he asked, already backing out.

"The Gem Shop."

"The Gem Shop?"

"Perry received an anonymous gift today that has him a little freaked out. It came from the store."

"Another secret admirer present?"

"I guess, but this time the admirer really is secret." I told him how Perry had sent all the other presents to himself. And now he was over the moon because Mario couldn't remember their big fight.

Kevin laughed. It had been a while since I'd heard the sound, and I suddenly remembered how much I liked it.

How much I liked him.

I looked out the window as we drove past house after house. "How'd Delphine's hearing go?" It had been postponed until today when the news about the accident reached the courtroom yesterday.

"Not well for her."

"But—"

"I know what you're going to say, Nina, but if it looks like a duck and acts like a duck, then it's a duck. She had means and motive and the evidence is stacked against her."

I folded my arms. "Sometimes a duck is a loon."

He smiled. "Same family, right?"

I wasn't sure, so I kept my mouth shut.

"Look," he said, "I talked to Honey and checked hers and Jean-Claude's alibis. They're airtight."

"Did she admit to being the accident victim's sister?"

"Yes. She confessed to marrying Joey to ruin him. To make his life miserable, to take all his money, to turn evidence she discovered against him cheating homeowners over to police. She says she'd never kill him because she'd wanted him to live as long as possible in misery. Delphine wasn't kidding when she told us that Honey didn't like her husband. She didn't just not like him—she hated him. She gets the last laugh about it, too."

"Why's that?"

"Joey had an enormous life insurance policy taken out a month after they were married. She's the beneficiary."

"Um, hello! Motive!"

"Quack, quack, remember? Honey took a lie detector. Passed with flying colors. She's telling the truth."

This time. "Well, we know Delphine couldn't have tampered with the water heater. Did you talk to Plum?"

He stared out the front window. "She's absolutely devastated, Nina, and was barely coherent when we questioned her."

"She could be a good actress."

"My instincts say no."

I couldn't argue with his instincts—they were pretty good. "Any leads on who Joey had been arguing with when Mario arrived?"

"We went back to sweep the place for prints. There are a lot, so it's going to take a while."

"What about the carbon monoxide leak? Were there any prints on the water heater?"

"It had been wiped clean."

"It feels like too much of a coincidence that the two cases are unconnected."

"I agree," he said quietly. "But I've yet to find a link."

"Delphine seems to be the link. Someone is out to get her. Kill her lover, frame her, kill her crew..."

He said nothing, which told me he was at least thinking along those lines himself.

Good.

I rubbed my temples as he pulled into the jewelry store's parking lot. There was a truck parked there I recognized.

"Well, I'll be," I said.

"What?"

"Look!"

Kevin smiled. "Someone's going to be a happy girl."

I would have hopped out of Kevin's car and run into the store, but my head was pounding. Instead, I walked slowly, albeit with a spring in my step. Kevin held open the door, but just before going inside his cell phone rang. He said, "I need to take this. I'll be right in."

I left him outside and fairly floated into the shop. I walked up behind Kit and said, "Fancy seeing you here."

Kit frowned at me as he handed a credit card over to Saul. "What're you doing here?"

I grinned ear to ear. "What're *you* doing here? You're supposed to be in charge of casa chaos."

"I took a break," Kit said.

Saul rang the sale and slid the credit card receipt across the counter to be signed. "He's buying a lovely ring for his—" He cut himself off when Kit growled at him.

"It's okay, Saul. I know what he's doing, and it's about time."

Kit groaned. "Don't say a word, Nina. Don't breathe it, don't think it."

"Don't worry. Your secret's safe with me."

He took his bag. "Good. Now really, what're you doing here? You're supposed to be resting."

What was with people today? I wasn't an invalid. "Just a quick errand. " I took the cufflink box out of my pocket and slid it across the counter to Saul. "I need to know who sent these to Perry."

"Sorry, Nina, I can't divulge that information."

"Can't or won't?"

"My hands are tied."

The door behind me opened, and I turned to find Kevin coming inside, a sad look on his face.

Kit shook his head and said, "I've got to go." He practically ran out the door.

Kevin smirked. "He's in a rush."

"He doesn't do well with mush and gush." I smiled as I watched Kit hop into his truck. He zoomed away. I turned back to Kevin and quickly caught him up on the situation I was facing. "Saul's hands are tied. He won't reveal who sent the cufflinks." I wiggled my eyebrows and jerked my chin toward Saul. I needed Kevin to pull rank.

The corner of his lip twitched, then he cleared his throat. "Saul, these cufflinks are part of an ongoing investigation," Kevin bluffed. "We need that information."

Saul's eyes widened. "I can't. It's against store policy."

Kevin shrugged. "I could come back with a warrant. And the store might need to be closed down for a few days..."

A bead of sweat popped out of Saul's forehead. "Okay, okay!" He rifled through a drawer and pulled out a receipt book. He frowned. "It was a cash order."

"So, no name?"

"I always take a name. It was—" he took out his glasses and squinted at the page, "Joe Smith."

It might have well been John Doe.

Kevin said, "Small guy, dark coloring, clean-cut, and a nervous kind of demeanor?"

Saul nodded vigorously. "Yes, yes! That's him. He came in with Donatelli Cabrera two nights ago."

Mario. That sneaky little... I glanced at Kevin. "How'd you know?"

"Seemed like something he would do."

Saul wiped his forehead. "He said something about the cufflinks being an expensive makeup gift, but Donatelli talked him into buying them to show the 'depth of his feelings.'" He used air quotes and rolled his eyes.

I had a feeling that Saul was more about the moolah than the emotion of his business.

Bear Broward must have gotten through to Mario that day in the basement. Well, with a little push from Mr. Cabrera as well. I thought it hysterical that Mario turned the tables on Perry and sent the gift anonymously. Perry was going to be thrilled he could keep the cufflinks.

Then I recalled that Mario wasn't going to remember sending them.

"Thanks, Saul," I said, tucking the cufflinks back into my pocket. As Kevin and I walked outside, his face was still somber. "What was that call? Not Mario..."

"No," he said. "Plum. She's in the hospital—she tried to kill herself."

I let out a long sigh as Kevin drove me home. "Did you get a prognosis?"

"Not yet. There's something else, too."

"What?"

"The prints from Joey and Honey's place. We got an interesting match on one set from the back door, thanks to you."

"Me? Why? How? Whose?"

"Ethan Onderko. And the only reason his prints were in

the database was because you had Tam enter them."

"Ethan? What did Ethan have to do with Joey?"

Kevin said, "I don't know. But I'm going to find out. He's still in the hospital, so I need to head over there." He pulled up in front of my house and leaned over, like he was going to kiss me. Instead, he tucked a strand of my hair behind my ear. "Good job, Nina."

I hopped out of the car and watched him drive away, telling myself that I hadn't wanted him to kiss me.

But I had a firm commandment in place about not deluding myself, so I let the truth wash over me.

I wanted the kiss.

Sue me.

Chapter Twenty-five

Before I went inside, I crossed the street to take a look at the progress in Mario and Perry's back yard. No one catcalled *me* when I made my way through the gaggle of Kit's colorful friends.

I tried not to take it personally.

I followed the side of the house and paused to take in the scene. My crew had outdone themselves.

Kit nodded when he saw me as though I hadn't just run into him at the jewelry store fifteen minutes ago. He stood close to me and looked around. "Not too bad."

"Not bad at all." My design had come to life. Everything was perfect from the simplest annual to the fabric on the lounge chairs on the new sun deck. Someone had even power-washed and stained the existing deck off the back of the house and covered it with a pergola that added a touch of something extra special. "It's wonderful. Mario and Perry are going to be thrilled. You did a great job, Kit. Everyone did."

"It was your design."

"And the hard work of you and the crew."

He shifted uncomfortably. "This love fest is making me a little queasy."

"Me, too."

"That's probably the concussion. I know you love the mushy stuff."

"You think you know me so well."

"I don't?"

I stuck my tongue out at him. "I'm going home."

"It's about time."

I glanced up at the sky, at the clouds rolling in. "Storm's coming."

"We're finishing up. The inside is almost done, too. Another couple of days, and it'll be good as new."

I wanted to tell him how special I thought he was for pulling this off, but even though I was a mushy kind of girl, he definitely wasn't a mushy kind of guy. I spoke his language instead. "Have I given you a raise lately?"

He laughed, a deep rumble. "No, and I'll need one, what with the—"

"Wedding to plan?" I finished.

"Weren't you leaving?"

I leaned up and kissed his cheek. He wiped it away. "Have you lost your mind? Not in front of everyone!"

I laughed. "Blame it on the concussion." I started walking toward home, but turned around. "And Kit?"

"What?" he snapped.

"Welcome to the family."

I could have sworn he smiled.

But it might just have been a trick of the light.

***

The storm hit just after sunset. Gracie trembled under the covers on the couch as lightning lit the sky beyond the windows and thunder shook the house.

I surfed the web as Maria watched *Miss Congeniality*. I thought she'd officially lost her mind with all this pageant stuff.

There had been no word from Kevin since I saw him off earlier this afternoon, but Riley had dropped by to whup me in a game of Scrabble. I tried to blame the loss on my scrambled brain, but the truth was I had a lot on my mind and couldn't focus.

Plus, he was a Scrabble shark, having learned at the knee of Mr. Cabrera.

Speaking of, he'd come over for dinner, picked at the pizza I'd ordered in, and left again. There still hadn't been any word from Brickhouse.

Perry was with Mario at the hospital, but would be back soon to get a good night's sleep. He'd broken into tears when I told him who'd sent the cufflinks.

I wasn't entirely sure whether it was because of the sentiment behind the gift—or because he got to keep the cufflinks.

I'd been reading and re-reading Ethan Onderko's file that Tam had sent me. It was as plain and boring as it had been before. Did he have something to do with Joey's death? Had Ethan been pushed to the edge after his fight with Joey the morning he died?

Over Joey being *slobby*? It didn't make sense.

Because the files were open, I went over Honey's and Bear's as well. There was something there that kept nagging at me, something big, but I couldn't focus enough to put it together.

Sighing, I closed the laptop and set it on the table.

Maria said, "This is my favorite part. The big makeover reveal. Look, look!"

I had to laugh at her exuberance as Sandra Bullock strutted across the screen, then I froze as the lights flickered.

The wind howled, and I went in search of flashlights in case the power went out. And I started worrying about all the new plantings across the street.

I was halfway to the kitchen when the house went dark.

Maria whispered, "I never did like the dark."

Me, either.

I found a flashlight in the drawer and flicked it on. I said, "Maybe we should head to bed. Sleep through this."

"Are you nuts? Do you really think we can sleep through this?"

Just as she said it, the tornado siren started blaring.

Maria and I froze for a second. It was a Midwesterner's eternal debate...heed the siren or stick it out, hoping the warning wasn't for our neighborhood.

But as I'd just set a new commandment about heeding weather warnings, I said, "Come on. The closet down here is the safest place. I'll get Gracie."

"I'll grab the donuts."

"The donuts?"

"In case we get hungry," she said as though I were the densest person on earth.

I picked up Gracie and my cell phone, and also grabbed two bottles of water from the dark fridge. Donuts tended to make me thirsty.

We'd just settled in the dark closet when a text message came in for me from Riley. *In downstairs bathroom. Don't worry.*

He knew me well.

The wall behind my back vibrated from the force of the winds rattling the house.

Maria said, "When was the last time you cleaned out this closet?"

"Two, three years ago."

"Ugh! I hope I don't pick up some strange infection or something from being in here." She pushed aside a pair of my old work boots. Not the ones Mr. Cabrera had upchucked on—those had gone into the trash.

Fortunately, the closet was large, or else Maria would probably be sitting on my lap. As it was, she was sitting so close to me that I could feel her inhales and exhales.

Gracie continued to tremble on my lap, and no amount of my soothing would calm her. She hated storms.

Absently, I wondered about Kit and Ana and BeBe. If they were huddled together in a closet. Kit would have his hands full with Ana and her fear of small spaces and BeBe with her drool.

Nate texted Maria, and she sent a note back to him that she was fine except for being stuck in a closet with me.

"There are worse places," I said.

"Where?" she demanded.

Thunder cracked.

"At Kit's for one. BeBe drools."

Maria shuddered.

"See," I said. "And ew! Gracie just peed all over me." Maybe drool was better.

"Nina?"

"What?" I said, trying to scoot out of the wetness.

"That wasn't Gracie."

I aimed the flashlight at her face.

"My water just broke."

"Ohmygod! Oh. My. God. Ohmygod. We have to call for help. We have to get you to the hospital. I can't drive. You can't drive. Who's going to drive?"

Maria started laughing. Great big belly laughs. Literally.

"What's so funny?"

"You! *Ohmygod*," she mocked, still laughing.

My lips twitched and next thing I knew, I was laughing, too. And that's just what we were doing when the closet door flew open, and I stared at a pair of men's shoes. I aimed the flashlight upward and found a dripping wet Kevin peering down at us.

Maria and I burst out laughing again.

"What's so funny?" he asked, crouching down. "Move over."

"Trust me, you don't want to come in here. We need to go."

"Why's the floor wet?" He looked at his hand—that had touched the floor—then he looked up. "Does the roof have a leak?"

"No," I giggled. "Maria does."

Maria laughed and laughed.

Kevin stared at his hand in horror.

"We need to get Maria to the hospital. Her water broke."

"First," he said, heading to the bathroom, "I need to wash my hand. Twice."

"And I need to call Nate," she said, suddenly not sounding so amused.

I should probably change, too, since I was soaked. I ran upstairs and tried to find something to wear in the dark. I didn't care what it looked like as long as it was dry. I wobbled a little bit, feeling lightheaded, and took the stairs slower on the way down.

Rain blasted the roof, the windows. Lightning lit the sky almost constantly, giving the house an eerie glow.

I threw several towels into the downstairs closet along with one of my sweatshirts and nestled Gracie on top of them. I set a bowl of water in there and leaned down close to her face to tell her why we had to leave.

She blinked at me, still trembling.

Damn it. I couldn't leave her here. I used the flashlight beam to find a duffle bag at the top of the closet. I set my sweatshirt inside, and then Gracie. I left the top half-zipped so she could have plenty of air.

Kevin had gone out and retrieved his extra large industrial strength flashlight from the car. It was practically like having a light on in the house. He eyed the bag warily but didn't say anything.

Maria let out a soft moan.

Kevin said, "The contractions started while you were upstairs." He took the duffle from me. "I'll handle this. You handle Maria." He strode out the door.

I grabbed a raincoat from the laundry room. "Ready?"

"Hell no!"

"I meant right this minute, not in the general sense of becoming a mother."

"Hell no!"

"Come on," I said, "before another contraction."

Solemnly, she nodded. I held the raincoat over her head, took her arm, and helped her down the steps and into Kevin's

SUV.

For the second time in two days he used his lights and sirens on a drive to the hospital. Only this time, the ride was painfully slow—not because of his concern for Maria but because the roads were quickly flooding and the drenching rain made it incredibly hard to see.

I glanced over at Maria. By the glow of the lightning I could see her anxiety. I put my arm around her. "It'll be okay."

"Promise?" she said.

I held up my baby finger. "Pinkie swear."

Chapter Twenty-six

Nate had beaten us to the hospital, and I gladly turned my sister over to her husband. The hospital was running on generators, and the hallways were dimmer than normal. The nurses kicked Kevin and I out of Maria's room while they got her settled in, registered, and hooked up to monitors.

Kevin and I stood outside Maria's door. He said, "Are you wearing one of my shirts?"

I looked down. I had grabbed an old shirt of Kevin's along with plaid flannel pajama pants. I'd stolen the shirt when he'd been living at my house for a while after being shot in the line of duty. It wasn't one of my prouder moments, but it had been too hard to resist. "I think it's one of my old ones."

"It looks like one of mine."

"You need to get your eyes checked."

He smiled. I smiled.

"My baby sister is going to have a baby," I said softly.

Scooting closer to me, he said, "You're going to be a great aunt."

I scrunched my nose. "Do you think I'd be a good mom?"

His mouth dropped open. "Geez! Are you pregnant?"

At the shock on his face, I laughed. "No! I'm just wondering. I think about it sometimes. Having a baby..."

He sagged against the wall in apparent relief. His eyes softened when he looked at me. "I've said it before, and I'll say it again. You *are* a good mom. Just ask Riley."

Before I could get mushy, Nate popped out of the room looking terrified. "She's already six centimeters dilated. The anesthesiologist is on the way up, and after that you can come back in."

He ducked back into the room.

"Coffee?" Kevin said.

"We're going to need it. I mean, that is, if you're staying."

"I'm staying."

I tried to hide the goofy smile on my face as we headed to the cafeteria. The stairs were eerily dark, lit only with small emergency lights along the bottom of the steps. Our footfalls echoed.

"Maria's labor is going fast," Kevin said. "I hope they're ready."

"They're ready."

"And I hope they've already set up a college fund for the baby. I was looking into costs for Riley in a year, and I think I should have chosen a life of crime instead of law."

College. I grabbed his arm. "College!"

Warily, he studied me. "Right. College..."

"You don't understand." College had been the thing in the files that had been eluding me these past two days. I quickly explained to Kevin. "I was thinking to myself how Honey's and Ethan's backgrounds were so similar, except for the loss of Honey's brother. They're similar in age, have clean records, and my brain just realized they went to the same college." I shoved him a little bit. "The same college! And they both moved to Cincinnati at the same time. I'd bet my last roll of cookie dough that they know each other." *You love her, don't you?* "Maybe better than any of us dreamed."

His eyes darkened. "Delphine did say that it was Joey who brought Ethan onto the crew."

"Undoubtedly Honey finagled that somehow."

I leaned against the wall. "Did she mastermind this whole thing? The life insurance, having an airtight alibi when her husband was killed..."

Oh my God, Jean-Claude. How did he fit into this mess?

The cafeteria was quiet as we filled cardboard mugs with stale coffee. "Did you interview him earlier? What did he have to say about his prints at the house?"

"I couldn't find him. He'd been discharged from the hospital, and he wasn't at home. I have patrol looking for him."

You love her, don't you?

"You realize he's probably the guy Mario heard in the house with Joey, right?" My mouth dropped open and I latched onto Kevin's shirt as another realization hit me hard.

His gaze dropped to my hand, clutching a fistful of cotton.

"Mario," I whispered. "He tried to kill Mario, too."

"Nina, that's quite a leap."

"No, no. It makes perfect sense. Mario said he recognized the voice in Joey's house but couldn't place it. What if Ethan was scared he eventually would? On the day the water heater was installed, Mario was supposed to spend the night at the house, but at the last minute decided to stay another night with Kit. If Ethan tinkered with the water heater before he left, he probably figured Mario would be a goner by the morning."

"And when he showed up and Mario wasn't dead?"

"Let's just say it probably wasn't a coincidence that Ethan was working in a space with good ventilation and took lots of smoke breaks. He probably wasn't too concerned about the collateral damage."

Because he was a killer.

My instincts had been vindicated, but this wasn't the time to gloat. "Mario's still in danger."

"Let me make some calls. I'll get hospital security up to Mario's room right away, and a security detail here as soon as possible. And I might have to leave after all. I need to have a talk with Honey."

I bit the inside of my cheek as he wandered off to find better cell phone coverage. My stomach churned, and I ended up dumping my coffee.

Kevin was back a minute later. "I need to go."

"Let me get Gracie from your car."

The rain had let up, but it was still drizzling. The worst of the storm had passed to the east, but I had a feeling the aftermath of what it had left behind wouldn't truly be revealed 'til morning.

Kevin clicked his keychain to unlock the doors, and reached in for the duffle. He'd left the windows down an inch for air circulation for Gracie, and the upholstery was soaked, but he didn't seem to mind. He handed the bag over to me, and I peeked inside. Gracie was sound asleep.

Footsteps caught my attention and I looked up as a doctor in blue scrubs, a white lab coat, and a surgical mask pulled up over his chin walked by, heading into the hospital. I squinted after him.

Kevin dropped a kiss on my cheek and headed for the driver's door. Suddenly, I grabbed onto his shirt again.

"You really have to stop doing that," he said, staring at my hand.

"That doctor who just walked by... The scrubs threw me off, but I'm pretty sure it was Ethan, Kevin."

"You're sure?"

The more I thought about it, the more I was sure. I'd seen Ethan at Perry and Mario's wearing a dust mask and the look was similar. "Yes! Go, go! Hurry!"

Kevin sprinted off. I tried to keep up, but Gracie and my headache were slowing me down. My heart pounded. Ethan had to be going after Mario. I could only hope that hospital security was already at Mario's room.

261

I chugged up the stairs and stopped on the maternity floor to drop off Gracie. I didn't want to go into Maria's room and have to explain everything, so I opened the door, shoved the duffle bag inside and quickly closed it again.

Maria's voice echoed down the hallway as I ran for the stairs. "*Neee-naaah!*"

Breathing hard, I raced up the steps. On Mario's floor, I flung open the stairwell door, took three strides down the hallway, and nearly collided with Ethan, who'd been sprinting for the stairway.

His eyes widened when he recognized me, and suddenly he didn't look like a creepy serial killer anymore but a scared kid.

Footsteps pounded, coming toward us. Ethan threw a look over his shoulder, then sprinted straight at me, grabbing my arm and twisting it behind my back before I could even think to react. He pulled me against his chest to use as a human shield just as Kevin and two uniformed guards turned the corner, guns drawn.

Ethan pressed something to my neck, and I could just barely make out that it was a syringe.

My knees went weak, but Ethan kept a firm grip on me. "Not another step!" he said to the men.

"Let her go, Ethan," Kevin said in a firm voice.

"No way."

I noticed that Kevin wouldn't look at me. Cool and calm, he kept his gaze squarely on Ethan.

My pulse jumped wildly in my throat, and I tried to calm

down a little. Get a grip on the situation. Figure a way out of it.

"Listen," Kevin said. "You're not too far into this that you can't get out."

I thought that was a bit of a stretch. Ethan had been responsible for killing three people. Possibly four.

Tears stung my eyes as I thought about Mario. I hoped and prayed that Ethan had been thwarted before carrying out his plan to kill Mario.

"You're not to blame, here." Kevin's voice soothed. "You were duped by Honey to do her dirty work. Put the syringe down, and let's talk about making a deal."

"Leave Honey out of this," Ethan seethed.

"Sorry, I can't. She used you, Ethan, plain and simple. She's used you, and she's going to let you take the fall while she picks up her life and moves on with a whole lot of cash and a brand-new lover."

"You're wrong! She loves me!"

I felt Ethan's body tense and hoped Kevin wouldn't push him too far. The prick of the needle on my neck kept digging a little deeper into my skin, in direct relation to Ethan's agitation.

"Yeah, she loves you so much she had you kill her husband."

"He deserved to die."

"And frame an innocent woman."

"She's not so innocent, is she?" he sneered.

"And to make sure she had an alibi when you made that call

to Joey to lure him to his death so her hands would be clean. She had a relationship with another man as a cover."

"He doesn't mean anything to her."

The needle jabbed harder, and I closed my eyes. I'd been up close and personal with death and killers before, and decided I'd never understand the psychosis behind their actions. Honey had sought revenge against Joey, yes, but in doing so she became no better than he was, maybe worse, because she had used Ethan to bring her plan to fruition.

Ethan started walking backward, toward the stairs. "Don't follow us. Or else."

I opened my eyes to find Kevin's gaze directly on mine. It narrowed and he looked toward the floor, then gave an almost imperceptible nod.

He wanted me to drop.

Easy for him to say.

Taking a deep breath, I pretended to stumble when Ethan took another step backward. Swinging my arm back, I hit him where the sun don't shine, and let my body go slack. I hit the floor like a sack of flour, and looked up in time to see Ethan bringing his hand down to stab me with the syringe.

I threw my hands up in defense and let out a scream as a single gunshot sounded. Blood splattered over me like a surreal rain shower as Ethan dropped the syringe and crumpled next to me, crying out and cradling his shoulder.

In a blink, Kevin was next to me, cradling me against his chest as the uniformed officers took care of Ethan. Hospital staff and curious patients filtered into the hallway.

Kevin's heart beat wildly against my cheek, and he held my so tightly I could barely breathe. "You're okay," he said softly.

I knew I was. Thanks to him.

"Mario?" I asked.

"Fine. The security guards stopped Ethan from getting into the room."

I let out the breath I'd been holding. What a nightmare this was.

Tucking my hair behind my ear, Kevin let me go. "Let's get you cleaned up."

I could barely look at myself. "There's blood on your shirt."

He cupped my face and looked at me tenderly. "I thought you said it was your shirt."

"I lied."

He laughed and pulled me back into his arms, hugging me tightly. "Don't worry, I know where you can get another one."

I let him hold me like that for a long, long time.

Chapter Twenty-seven

A few days later, a full moon cast bountiful light over Mario and Perry's back yard. It was a glorious night, warm and balmy, perfect for a party. A slight breeze ruffled the leaves of the newly planted trees, and swished the long grasses along the fence and decks. On a night like tonight it was easy to imagine nothing but clear skies ahead.

People milled through the yard, talking under giant red lanterns, gathering around the food tent, and dancing in the moonlight. Peppy music couldn't quite drown out the sound of the crickets, but their incessant chirps only added to the festivities.

Perry hadn't left Mario's side since the party started—they were camped across from me on the sun deck, sharing a loveseat. They were in deep conversation with several neighbors, gossiping about the newly sold house next door to mine and what kind of neighbors might be moving in. No one knew, and it was driving everyone crazy.

Mario had been home for only a day and had no recollection of the horrible things that had happened here. Of the danger he'd been in. No one filled him in. Personally, I hoped those memories would forever be erased.

Tonight was all about celebrating. A homecoming. A new engagement. And a new baby.

Life.

The party had been thrown together at the last minute, and I decided those were my favorite kind of celebrations. There had been no invitations, no RSVPs, no pretensions, just a lot of people helping Mario create a *wonderful* new memory.

"She looks good on you," Kevin said, stepping up onto the platform and taking the chair next to mine. "Maybe not as good as a wet T-shirt, but it's close."

Moonbeams fell across his face, highlighting the humor in his eyes—and the hint of heat, too. I continued rocking, holding my brand-new niece against my shoulder. Her name was Vivienne Celeste, her middle name after my mother, which had immediately silenced my mother's very vocal long-distance distress over having missed the birth. Her nickname was Vivi, and I loved her with all my heart. I pressed my cheek against the warmth of her blond downy head and inhaled her sweet baby scent. "She does, doesn't she?"

With a soft touch, Kevin reached over and pushed aside a lock of loose hair that had fallen across my cheek, tucking the strand behind my ear. His hand then went to Vivi's head, cupping it oh-so-gently. "I was wrong. She is better than the wet T-shirt."

"Kevin Quinn, you big ol' softie."

"Don't let it get around."

Maria hovered nearby, casting furtive glances my way. She'd planned to stay only for a few minutes since a party wasn't the best place for a newborn. She was here long enough to show off her new daughter, collect some presents, and then be on her way with Nate.

One of my gifts to Vivi had been a toddler basketball set. Maria had immediately asked for the receipt.

Gracie was still staying with me. I wasn't quite sure why—or for how long—but I wasn't arguing with it, either. I liked the company.

I smiled at Ana as she and Kit danced on the lawn, laughing as he spun her around and dipped her low. Soft light from a lantern glinted off her new ring, making it sparkle like a bright star in a murky night sky.

I'd never seen her so happy, and I couldn't be happier for her. She deserved it. "They look good, don't they?"

"Yeah. They do." He leaned back in his chair, drew his right ankle onto his left knee and crossed his arms behind his head. "So, do you have plans for the weekend? You don't have a date with the coroner guy, do you?"

Even though he tried to make the question sound casual, I heard the serious undertone. "Not this weekend."

"I guess I deserved that," he said.

I didn't disagree. I thought about Cain. *Seth*. I'd received the all-clear from Ian yesterday. There was no threat on Seth's life. I didn't know what to do with the news and finally decided I'd take a wait-and-see approach. I didn't want to turn Seth's life upside down. It was enough for me to know he was alive. He was well. "And no, no plans other than to sleep and try to forget this past week."

Ethan was still under guard in the hospital recovering from the gunshot wound to his shoulder. The charges against him were numerous, pretty much guaranteeing the death penalty should he not make a deal to squeal on Honey.

So far, he wasn't squealing. In fact, he denied she had anything to do with what had gone down. That he acted alone. That she didn't even know him that well and that he was an obsessed stalker.

Honey, of course, denied everything, too. The police were trying their best to tie her to the crime, but at best their case was circumstantial. And it was a weak case at that. She'd covered her tracks well.

Jean-Claude also refused to believe she was involved. They were still dating.

Delphine had been released from jail and hadn't left her sister's side. As soon as Plum was well enough she would be transferred to a mental health facility.

It never ceased to amaze me what kind of damage grief could do to a person.

I didn't want to think about any of it anymore, so I said, "Why do you ask? Does Riley have something going on?"

He laughed. "Oh, he has something going on, all right. He has a date. He's meeting Layla's parents."

I shot him a look. "Have you met Layla?"

"Not yet. I get the feeling he doesn't want her to meet us."

I smiled—I'd voiced the same concern. "I can't imagine why."

Kevin laughed. "But it's because he's busy that I need some help."

Vivi gurgled and wiggled, and I set my hand on her back to soothe her. She'd yet to unfurl her body for any longer than a second, remaining curled up in a jelly bean shape. She was the cutest little lump I'd ever seen. "Help? With what?"

"Packing."

"Packing? Are you going on a trip? Something for work?"

Uncrossing his arms, he stretched them out. "I'm moving."

Every nerve ending in my body seized, and I stiffened. "Moving? Where?" Riley was already farther away than I liked. And of course, I had no say in where Riley lived. He wasn't my biological child. A child of my heart, yes, but that wasn't going to hold up in a court of law.

I was working myself into quite a tizzy when I heard Perry say, "I hope the new neighbor is nice eye candy. Someone who mows with his shirt off."

Mario nodded, playing along. "Someone who looks like Mark Consuelos would be nice. Ha cha cha!"

Perry laughed. "I'm okay with that."

I tipped my head as I looked between Perry and Kevin, Kevin and Perry.

Moonlight lit the mischievous spark in Kevin's eyes. A confirmation if I ever saw one. "You didn't."

"Someone has to restore law and order to this neighborhood."

Dumbfounded, I continued rocking.

"Now, I can't guarantee I'll mow shirtless, but if you ask me nicely... I might consider it. I wouldn't be opposed to you mowing shirtless, either, but then I'd be encouraging the unlawfulness and disorder around here, and that probably wouldn't do."

I didn't know what to think about this turn of events. On one hand, Riley was moving in next door. Next door! It was almost as good as living with me. But on the other hand, Kevin was moving in next door. And I wasn't sure how I felt about that at all.

"So?" he asked. "You think you'll have time to help me pack?"

I glanced over at him, feeling like I was agreeing to much more. So much more. "I can spare some time."

His head dipped in a subtle nod. "Good."

I caught a flash of movement and looked up in time to see Maria headed my way. "Nina, you're becoming a baby hog."

"Can you blame me?" I asked.

A smile spread across her face, making her glow from within. "Not at all. But it's time for us to go."

Gently, I shifted the little jelly bean into her mother's hands. Instinctively Maria curled her arms upward, protecting

Vivi. I already missed the flutter of her heartbeat against my chest.

"Maria," Perry said, "I just heard about a beautiful baby contest running in the paper. You should enter little Vivi."

Slowly, Maria shook her head. "Not yet."

I knew that tone. She meant not ever.

Maria saw me watching her. She shrugged. "I don't really like the idea of strangers having easy access to her."

"But the pageants..." I said.

"Oh!" She lit up. "I had the best idea. A granny pageant! We can hold it here in the Mill, get the neighbors involved."

"Dear Lord," Kevin muttered.

Perry clapped. "I'll help!" Maria crossed the deck to talk details with Perry.

"They're joking, right?" Kevin asked.

"I don't think so."

"Riley's never going to bring Layla around, is he?"

"Doubtful."

"I need a drink. You?"

I nodded and stood up. "I'll get them. I want to check on Mr. Cabrera."

He sat opposite us, near the outdoor fireplace in a chair next to the libation station. He had a glass in his hand that looked suspiciously like a cocktail and a dour look on his face. He wore a plain polo shirt and drab gray shorts.

The sun had gone down on Mr. Cabrera.

I sat next to him and said, "Are you hungry? There's plenty of food."

"No. Thanks."

"Is that gin you're drinking?" I checked what shoes I had on—cheap flip flops—and let out a breath of relief.

"It's a Manhattan. Perry made it for me."

I gave Perry the Ceceri Evil Eye, but he was oblivious as he chatted with Maria. "He's a bad influence."

"Nah. He's okay."

I wasn't sure what to say to cheer him up. There was no denying the obvious—that Brickhouse hadn't come back when she heard Mr. Cabrera had been in the hospital. And she had heard—her daughter Claudia confirmed it.

"I asked her, you know," he said.

"To marry you?"

He nodded. "The morning after she left. She was so mad she wouldn't even open the door. I had to slide the ring through the mail slot."

I bit my cheek to keep from smiling. This wasn't a humorous situation, but that visual...I wanted to laugh. "Did she slide it back out?"

With a sudden jerk, he faced me full-on. "Are you laughing?"

Pressing my lips together, I shook my head.

"No, she did not. She kept it. Said she'd think about what I said while she was away and give me an answer when she came back."

"So she didn't say no."

"But she didn't come back when I was in the hospital, either."

Yeah, that was pretty bad. "Well," I said, trying to spin it, "she was really upset with you, rightfully so. You've been taking her for granted."

"You're quite the cheer squad," he muttered.

"And by the time she heard you were in the hospital, you were already home and doing fine."

He shrugged and grumbled.

"Look, do you have email?"

"Like on the computer?"

"Yes, that's usually how it's done."

"No. I don't even have a computer."

Glittering stars twinkled overhead. "We need to get you a laptop. And you're going to start emailing Ursula every day, telling her how much you love her and miss her."

"I am?"

"You are. You're going to stop moping, accept responsibility for your actions, and start making up for them. It's never too late to right a wrong. You'll beg for a second chance, a third if needed. You'll do everything it takes because love isn't something that comes along everyday and you should be thanking your lucky stars you have it at all."

He perked up a little. "Never too late, eh?"

"Never."

"A computer, you say."

I nodded.

He puffed up. "I'll give it a try. On one condition."

"What's that?"

He motioned behind me. "That you take your own advice, Miz Quinn."

I glanced over my shoulder, found Kevin watching me intently. Heat flooded my neck, my ears. "That's not what I—"

Mr. Cabrera wagged a finger at me. "A deal's a deal."

"You don't play fair."

Chuckling, he stood. "I play to win." Reaching out, he held out his hand for a shake. "Do we have a deal?"

I remembered the thought I had as I watched Mrs. Krauss drive away last week.

Sometimes looking ahead meant not looking behind you.

Reluctantly, I shook. "The things I do for you."

He kept chuckling as he walked away.

Kevin came up behind me. "What was that all about?"

"A deal with the devil," I muttered, pulling a cold beer out of a tin bucket for him, and a Dr Pepper for me. As much as I wanted something harder, I was still taking medication for the concussion.

Next to me, I felt Kevin straighten. "Nina?"

"Yeah?" I popped the top on the can and slurped my way around the edge.

"You sure you didn't have plans with the coroner guy?"

I sighed. "Look, you have to stop bringing him up, your jealousy's making me cranky. You don't understand what's going—"

I felt a tap on my shoulder. "Nina?"

Kevin's lips tightened in smugness.

Slowly, I turned. Cain Monahan stood behind me. I coughed a little, liquid caught in my throat.

Kevin thumped my back—a little harder than necessary, I thought.

Cain said, "Sorry to interrupt. Can I talk to you for a second?"

Glancing at Kevin out of the corner of my eye, I could feel the heat in my cheeks.

"Why don't you tell me what's going on then?" Kevin asked softly.

I ground my teeth. Suddenly my deal with Mr. Cabrera felt quite daunting. "Second chances," I muttered.

Kevin leaned in. "What was that?"

"I'm sorry," Cain said, glancing between us. "I can come back later."

"No," I said to him. "Now's fine." I jabbed Kevin's chest. "I'll talk to you later."

He caught my hand and stared into my eyes. "I'm not going anywhere, Nina. I'm here to stay."

My heart hammered. "I figured."

Giving a curt nod, he walked away.

Cain said, "Is he always that intense?"

"No. Sometimes, he's worse."

Cain smiled, and my heart melted at the familiarity of it.

He said, "He seems rather...attached to you."

I didn't really want to think about Kevin right now. I walked over to a quieter corner of the yard. Cain followed. I said, "You wanted to talk to me?"

His brown eyes looked black in the dim lighting, but the flecks of gold flashed. "I feel strange even coming to you, but..."

"What?" I asked, letting him lead.

"Look, I'm just going to lay it on the line, okay?"

"Lay away."

The skin on his brow wrinkled as he frowned deeply, his eyebrows dipping, his lips pulling low. His gaze met mine dead on. The darkness couldn't mask the emotion I saw flickering in the depths.

"I don't know who I am," he said, his voice shaking. "But I have the feeling you do."

A lump formed in my throat, and I bit the inside of my cheek. "Do I know you? I do. You're a ghost. A memory. A miracle. The ultimate second chance. And you've been dead for twenty years."

He blinked, and confusion clouded his eyes.

I linked arms with him. "Let's go for a walk, and I'll tell you all about a boy I used to know."

As we headed for the street, the beat of the music pulsated through the air and thrummed through my body. Yes, this party was about life. The living. The *good*.

"It's good to be alive, isn't it?" I said to him.

He tipped his head in the way I used to know so well. "You're a little strange, aren't you, Bo-bina?"

I laughed. "You used to know exactly how much. But now... Now you're going to learn all over again."

I'd lost him once and I wasn't going to let it happen a second time.

Moonlight lit the street as we wandered along. "Seth. You're name is Seth..."

From the Desk of Nina Quinn

Did you know that over the past few years outdoor fire features have become one of the most requested designs in a landscape? If you're longing for one, a fire pit is the perfect weekend project to tackle if you're a do-it-yourselfer. However, there are a few things to keep in mind before adding a fire pit to your backyard design.

It's a Material World

Fire pits can be as simple or complex as you desire. Your design will depend on a few factors including time, cost, and space. The go-to fire pit I use in my designs is almost always a simple metal bowl surrounded by a round or square decorative wall of brick or flagstone—materials found easily at your local garden center. Constructed much like a retaining wall, the surround is usually four to five courses of stone topped with capstone. A mallet, a level, a shovel, some landscape caulk or mortar, and you're well on your way to getting the job done. Throw in some logs and you'll be making s'mores in no time at all.

If you're looking for a fancier design, consider creating a gas fire pit using propane. It's a little more technical (plans are often available at your local garden center), but the use of decorative colored tumbled glass or lava rocks surrounding the flame ring looks spectacular.

Easy Does It

If you're looking for a quick and easy fix, check your local home store. Most sell freestanding fire pits (including gas pits), fire bowls, chimineas, and also prefab stone fire pit and fireplace kits. Prices vary to fit every budget.

Safety First

Safety is of the highest importance for any project. First things first, make sure you check your town or city codes. Some do not allow fire features due to the risk of wildfires and/or pollution concerns. While there, also check to see if you need a permit to construct a fire pit in your back yard. You don't want to put all the work into your project only to be told it needs to be torn down. Be sure to "Call before you dig" to check for underground electrical and gas lines. For the actual site of your feature, consider how the wind blows and keep your fire pit at least ten feet from flammable structures and always keep a hose or bucket of water handy in case your flames get out of control. Oh, and make sure none of the materials you use are combustible. River stones, for example, will explode when heated and never use pressure treated wood in your fire pit because it releases a toxin when burned.

Soon you'll be sitting in your yard, enjoying the results of your hard work. Alluring wood smoke and crackling flames will set the perfect back drop for a night of entertaining friends or a cozy night snuggled up with a loved one. Save me a s'more.

Best wishes for happy gardening!

About the Author:

Heather Webber (aka Heather Blake) is the author of more
than a dozen novels. She's a Dr Pepper enthusiast, total
homebody who loves to be close to her family, read, watch
Reality TV (totally addicted, especially to competition shows),
crochet, occasionally leave the house to hike the beautiful
mountains in the northeast, and bakes (mostly cookies).
Heather grew up in a suburb of Boston, but she currently lives
in the Cincinnati area with her family.

www.heatherwebber.com
www.heatherblakebooks.com

Read on for a sneak peek at the first book in
Heather Blake's new Magic Potion series,

A Potion to Die For

Coming in November 2013 from Obsidian

If there were a Wanted poster for witches, I was sure my
freckled face would be on it.

Ducking behind a tree to catch my breath, I sucked in a
deep lungful of humid air as I listened to the cries of the search
party.

I didn't have much time before the frenzied mob turned the
corner and spotted me, but I needed to take a rest or risk
keeling over in the street.

It was times like these that I wished I was the kind of witch
who had a broomstick. Then I could just fly off, safe and
sound, and wouldn't be hiding behind a live oak, my hair
sticking to its bark while my lungs were on fire.

But *noooo*. I had to be a healing witch from a long line of
hoodoo practitioners (and one rogue voodoo-er, but no need
to go into that this very moment). I was a love potion expert,
matchmaker, all- around relationship guru, and an unlikely
medicine woman.

Fat lot of good all that did me right now.

In fact, my magic potions were why I was in this

predicament in the first place.

I'd bet my life savings (which, admittedly, wasn't much) that my archnemesis, Delia Bell Barrows, had a broomstick. And though I had never before been envious of the black witch, I was feeling a stab of jealousy now.

Quickly glancing around, I suddenly hoped Delia lurked somewhere nearby—something she had been doing a lot of lately. I'd been trying my best to avoid a confrontation with her, but if she had a broomstick handy—and was willing to loan it to me— would be more than willing to talk.

There were some things worth compromising principles for, obviously. Like a rabid mob.

But the brick- paved road, lined on both sides with tall shade trees, was deserted. If Delia was around, she had a good hiding spot. Smart, because there was a witch hunt going on in the streets of Hitching Post, Alabama.

And I, Carly Hartwell, was the hunted witch.

Again.

This really had to stop.

Pushing off from the tree, I spared a glance behind me before running at a dead sprint through the center of town toward my shop, Little Shop of Potions, with the mob hot on my heels. The storefront was painted a dark purple with lavender trim, and the name of the shop was written in bold curlicue letters on the large picture window. Underneath was the shop's tagline: mind, body, heart, and soul. Behind the glass, several vignettes featuring antique glass jars, mortar and pestles, apothecary scales and weights I'd collected over the years filled the big display space.

At this point I should have felt nothing but utter relief. I was almost there. So . . . close.

But instead of relief, a new panic arose.

Because standing in front of my door was none other than Delia.

I could hardly believe it. Now she shows up.

I grabbed the store key and held it at the ready. "Out of the way, Delia!"

Delia stood firm, neck to toe in black—from her cape to her toenails, which stuck out from a pair of black patent flip-flops that had a skull- and- crossbones decoration. A little black dog, tucked into a basket like Toto, barked.

The dog was new. The cape, all the black, and the skull- and- crossbones fascination was not.

"I need to talk to you, Carly," Delia said. "Right now."

I hip checked Delia out of the way, and the dog yapped. Sticking the key into the lock, I said, "You're going to have to wait. Like everyone else." I threw a nod over my shoulder.

The crowd, at least forty strong, bore down.

Delia let out a gasp. "Did Mr. Dunwoody give a forecast this morning?"

"Yes." The lock tumbled, and I pushed open the door and scooted inside. Much to my dismay, Delia snuck in behind me.

I had two options: to kick the black witch out—which would then let the crowd in . . . or keep Delia in—and the crowd out.

Delia won.

Slamming the door, I threw the lock.

Just in time. Fists pounded the wood frame and dozens of eyes peered through the window.

I yelled through the leaded glass panel, "I'll be open in half an hour!" but the eager crowd kept banging on the door.

Trying to catch my breath, I walked over to the cash register counter, an old twelve- drawer chestnut filing cabinet. I opened one of the drawers and grabbed a small roll of numbered paper tickets. Walking back to the door, I shoved them through the wide mail slot.

"Take numbers," I shouted at the eager faces. "You know the drill!"

Because, unfortunately, this wasn't the first time this had happened.

Turning my back to the crowd, I leaned against the door, and then slid down its frame to the floor. For a second I rested against the wood, breathing in the comforting scents of my shop. The lavender, lemon balm, mint. The hint of peach leaf, sage, cinnamon. All brought back memories of my grandma Adelaide Hartwell, who'd opened the shop more than fifty years before.

"You should probably exercise more," Delia said. Her little dog barked.

My chest felt so tight I thought any minute it might explode. "I think I just ran a five- K. Second time this month."

"What exactly did Mr. Dunwoody's forecast say?"

"Sunny with a chance of divorce."

Delia peeked out the window. "That explains why there are so many of them. I wonder whose marriage is on the chopping block."

The matrimonial predictions of Mr. Dunwoody, my septuagenarian neighbor, were never wrong. His occasional "forecasts" foretold of residential current affairs, so to speak. On a beautiful spring Friday in Hitching Post, the wedding capital of the South, one might think a wedding ceremony—or a few dozen— was on tap. But it had been known, a time or two, for a couple to have a sudden change of heart over their recent nuptials (usually after the alcohol wore off the next morning) and set out to get the marriage immediately annulled or file for a quickie, uncontested divorce.

And even though Mr. Dunwoody was never wrong, I often wished he'd keep his forecasts to himself.

Being the owner of the Little Shop of Potions, a shop that specialized in love potions, was a bit like being a mystical bartender. People talked to me. A lot. About everything. Especially about falling in love and getting married, which was the height of irony considering everyone on my mother's side of the family were confirmed matrimonial cynics. Luckily, the hopeless romanticism on my father's side balanced things out for me. Mostly.

Somehow over the years I had become the town's unofficial relationship expert. It was at times rewarding . . . and a bit exasperating. The weight of responsibility was overwhelming, and I didn't always have the answers, magic potions or not.

Because Southerners embraced crazy like a warm blanket on a chilly night, not many here cared much that I called myself a witch, or that I practiced magic using a touch of hoodoo. But the town thought I did have all the answers—and expected me to find solutions.

My customers cared only about whether I could make their lives better. Be it an upset stomach or a relationship falling apart, they wanted healing.

And when there was a divorce forecast, they were relentless until I made them a love potion ensuring their marriage would be secure. I had a lot of work to get done. Work I'd rather not have done with Delia around.

"Why are you here?" I asked her.

"I had a dream," Delia said, fussing with her dog's basket.

"A Martin Luther King, Jr., kind? Or an REM- drool-on-the- pillow kind?" I asked, looking up at her.

"REM. But I don't drool."

"Noted," I said, but I didn't believe it for a minute. I shifted on the floor— y rear was going numb. "What was it about? The dream."

Delia said, "You."

"Me? Why?"

Delia closed her eyes and shook her head. After a dramatic pause, she looked at me straight on. "Don't ask me. It's not like I have any control over what I dream. Trust me. Otherwise, I'd be dreaming of David Beckham, not you."

I could understand that. "Why are you telling me this?" We weren't exactly on friendly terms.

Delia bit her thumbnail. All of her black- painted nails had been nibbled to the quick. "I don't like you. I've never liked you, and I daresay the feeling is mutual."

I didn't feel the need to agree aloud. I had some manners after all. "But?" I knew there was one coming.

"I felt I had to warn you. Because even though I don't like you, I don't particularly want to see anything bad happen to you."

Now I was really worried. "Warn me about what?"

Caution filled Delia's ice blue eyes. "You're in danger."

Danger of losing my sanity, maybe. This whole day had been more than a little surreal and it wasn't even nine a.m. I laughed. "You know this from a dream?"

"It's not funny, Carly. At all. I . . . see things in dreams. Things that come true. You're in very real danger."

She said it so calmly, so easily, that I immediately believed her. I'd learned from a very early age not to dismiss things that weren't easily understood or explainable.

"What kind of danger?" I asked. I'd finally caught my breath and needed a glass of water. I hauled myself off the floor and headed for the small break room in the back of the shop. I wasn't the least bit surprised when Delia followed.

"I don't know," she admitted.

I flipped on a light. And froze. Delia bumped into my back. We stood staring at the sight before us.

Delia said breathlessly, "It might have something to do with him."

"Him" being the dead man lying facedown on the floor, blood dried under his head, his stiff hands clutching a potion bottle.